The Empty City

a novel about Love, Games, and the planet Mars

by Andrew Looney

with illustrations by
Alison "Looney" Frane

cover painting by
Dawn Robyn Petrlik

Published by Looney Labs

PO Box 761, College Park, MD, 20740, USA

www.LooneyLabs.com

List of Alison's Illustrations

Copyright © 2002 by Looney Laboratories, Inc.
PO Box 761, College Park, MD, 20740, USA

ISBN # 1-929780-00-1
Item # LOO-016

The short story entitled "The Empty City" was first published by
Maryland Media, Inc. in the Spring 1986 edition of *Calvert*.
The first edition of this novel was published in 1991 by Icehouse Games, Inc.

Icehouse, Icehouse Pieces, The 100,000 Year Old Game From Mars,
Zarcana, and Martian Chess are all trademarks of Looney Labs, Inc.
All Rights Reserved.

Visit **www.LooneyLabs.com** *today!*

Table of Contents

To Kristin

For me, any city would be empty
if you weren't there to share it with.

Chapter 1

Early morning sunlight stabbed through the windows of an upstairs bedroom on the west side of the City. It was dawn, on the last day of summer.

Jennifer had slept very little that night, and when dawn finally broke she got out of bed. Jim rolled over and tried to continue sleeping, but found that he could not, and got up as well.

The room was rather barren. Jim's bed was just a single mattress on the floor, he didn't have a bed frame or a box spring. His only furniture was a busted up old couch and a small chair. He did have a desk, but he kept it in his walk-in closet.

Jennifer stood at the window, watching the sun rise. Jim went to the window and stood behind her. He put his hands on her shoulders, but she stiffened, and walked away.

"Are you still mad about last night?" asked Jim.

Jennifer sighed. "It's not just last night," she said quietly.

Jim sat down on the sofa. He suddenly felt very helpless. He tried to think of something to say, but could not. Jennifer sat down on Jim's chair and looked at him. For a long time they sat there, looking across at one another in silence. Finally, Jennifer stood up, and started getting dressed.

"Look, I have to go to work," she said.

"I know," said Jim, looking down at the floor.

After Jennifer had gone, Jim crawled back into bed, and worried.

Chapter 2

On the last day of summer, a cool breeze stirred the broiling air, and a small cloud drifted silently across the face of the sun. All over the city, people looked up at the sky with a sense of relief. The unbearably hot day was giving way to a pleasantly cool evening. As the sun beat a path toward the horizon, children went inside from their play, and adults went inside from their work. Dinners were served. TV sets began to bathe living rooms in pale bluish light.

At five minutes before seven that evening, four men sat down at a scraped-up old wooden table in an apartment on the tenth floor of a high rise on the east side of town. There they began to play a game of strategy, a game that had come to replace chess and backgammon as the standard board game for intellectual competition. It was called Icehouse.

The game of Icehouse was played on a free form surface—no board was required, only a flat area, such as a table top or floor. It could be played by two or more players, with no real upper limit, though most considered four the optimum number. The game employed the use of small four sided pyramids, of varying sizes and opposing colors, and was played by placing the pyramids out on the playing field. Once placed, it was rarely legal to move them, though this was permitted under certain conditions of the game. The game continued until all of the pyramids had been played.

The most important feature of Icehouse was that it happened in real time, that is, there was no sense of "turns." Anytime a player felt like making a move he could do so, provided it was a legal move. This meant that some phases of the game were met with frenzied activity by all players, and at other times, minutes would pass with little change in the playing surface, each person pleased with his position and carefully considering his options.

In games of more than two players, an important aspect was diplomacy. Two players might want to team up to defeat their opponents collectively and thus share a joint victory. Since it was much better strategically to work together without the knowledge of the enemy, there were often many elaborate signaling systems employed in a game of Icehouse.

Depending on the skill and style of the players, an Icehouse game could be as short as a minute, or as long as an hour. Therefore, most players used a timer of some sort to limit games to a 10 or 20 minute standard. (There were a few old-timers who enjoyed the endurance test presented by untimered Icehouse; for these players, the game was never suspended, no matter how important the phone call nor how urgent the need for restroom facilities.)

At five minutes before seven on the last evening of summer, four men sat down at a scraped-up old wooden table in an apartment on the tenth floor of a high rise on the east side of town. This group of men was known about town as The Four—a tightly knit group of friends who did everything together and who played Icehouse with intense savagery.

The Four were: Peter and Paul, the twins, who always wore matching clothes (a habit originally begun under duress, now a sort of fashion statement), Umberto, the fat man, usually called Bert, and Dave, who was, more or less, the leader of the group.

The game began with a controlled panic, each player dropping several of his pyramids into position rapidly. After ten seconds, each player slowly sat back, his pieces arranged in one of the usual opening positions.

Peter and Paul regarded each other from opposite sides of the table. Neither was sure how the game would end up. Much of the time, they teamed up to attack Bert and Dave, but this often became routine, and it was much more challenging for them to face off against each other. Since they thought the same way, it was very exciting when they tried to outguess each other. At this point, they were busy trying to decide which course to take.

Bert was especially pleased with his opening setup, and retrieved from under his chair a plastic tube containing ready-to-bake chocolate chip cookie dough. Raw cookie dough was one of Bert's favorite snacks. Using his thumb, he tore open the end of the plastic tube, and began scooping out big bites of the dough with a tarnished silver teaspoon.

Dave leaned back in his chair, and regarded the table and his opponents. He let his mind wander, and started pondering something more important than merely this game: the events of the coming night.

Peter and Paul looked at Bert and Dave. Bert was concentrating heavily on his roll of cookie dough, and Dave, though he was looking at the playing area, seemed to have his mind on something miles away. Almost simultaneously, the twins came to a decision: demolish the other two. They deserved it, since they weren't paying attention.

On a signal from Paul, they both leaned forward and began tossing pyramids onto the table. Bert growled through a mouthful of cookie dough, accidentally spitting out a chocolate chip. He tossed the roll of dough onto the floor, and grabbed at his stash of pyramids, getting them sticky in the process, quickly trying to make a few plays that would keep him from losing. But he was too late; the ambush had succeeded. Both Bert and Dave were already in the Icehouse.

Bert stood up, cursing and shouting at the twins about how badly he would beat them in the next game. Then he retrieved his tube of dough, now nearly half empty, and went into the kitchen in search of some milk.

Dave, who had not moved at all during his swift and utter defeat, said calmly, "Oh well, I guess we owe you."

The Four kept a chart on the wall that detailed who had won and lost each of their games. Each game carried with it a wager—the loser(s) owed the winner(s) a drink at the Saturn Cafe. Paul stood up and marked the new totals on the chart. "Hey," he said, "that game only lasted two minutes and thirteen seconds. That might be a new record."

"Big deal," said Bert as he returned with his milk. "What are we going to do tonight, anyway, just sit on our butts and Ice it?"

Dave stood up, as if to make an announcement. "I've been giving that some thought," he said, in his most pompous and dramatic voice. "I think it's time we did something with *that*." He pointed at a gray steel box in the corner.

"What, the atomic bomb?"

"Yes."

"Well... what? What can you do with an atomic bomb? Besides setting it off, I mean, and I don't think that's such a good idea."

"I was thinking about giving it away. It'd be the perfect gift for the man who has everything."

"Christmas is months from now. Besides, who'd want it?"

"The Android Sisters might like it."

"Now wait a minute," said Peter, standing up. "Bill made that bomb for me, remember? I don't recall saying that it was up for grabs."

"Oh, you don't want that old thing, Pete! You never use it, it's just gathering dust! Besides, you know as well as I do that Old Bill could never build a real atomic bomb. That's just a metal case with a big red button on the front."

"Now don't sell Bill short. I'll admit he's kind of a nut—but he's smart, too. I wouldn't be surprised if that thing there is an actual, working nuclear weapon. It took him long enough to make it."

"Right. Where would he get the plutonium?"

"At the hardware store, maybe. How should I know? All I know is that he said it's an atomic bomb, and since it's never been tested, I'm not going to doubt it."

"All right, all right, all right. Do you still want it, or not?"

"Well, I guess I can live without it. But you never know when you might need an atomic bomb."

"Look, we'll give it to the Android Sisters, I know they'll like it, and if you ever feel you need it, I'm sure they'll loan it to you."

"Well... OK."

"Great! Paul, see if you can find some wrapping paper." Dave lifted the atomic bomb out of its dusty spot in the corner and placed it in the center of the table. It was a gray steel box about a foot tall, a foot wide, and a foot and a half long. The various seams were closed with an excessive number of bolts; the designer clearly did not want the box opened. The words "ATOMIC BOMB" were stenciled in black along the top of the front panel. Below that, on the left, was a large red button labeled "DETONATION SWITCH: DO NOT PRESS." On the right were a number of small lights and a big red digital counter, above which were the words "SECONDS UNTIL DETONATION." Dave brushed a thin layer of dust off of the top, revealing a hand-painted radiation symbol and the words "HANDLE WITH CARE."

Presently, Paul arrived with the wrapping paper. "This is the best I could find," he said. It was light blue, and featured ducks and bunnies and birthday cakes with one candle and the words "HAPPY BIRTHDAY."

"It will have to do," said Dave.

As Dave was gift-wrapping the atomic bomb, the phone rang. Bert jumped up and went toward it, snarling at Paul, who started to answer it but then backed off.

Bert spoke into the mouth piece, "What!"

"Oh, hi Bert. This is Jim."

"It's Jim," Bert said to the others. Then, into the phone, "What's up?"

"Well, I figured I'd better let you know what just happened. Bill was just about to go to work when these three guys showed up and started asking him all these questions."

"What guys?"

"I don't know, they said they were from some atomic agency or something. They wanted to know why Bill had built an atomic bomb and what he'd done with it."

"And?"

"Bill said he'd given it to you guys."

"Great."

"I thought you should know. Be careful, dudes. They acted like they were the Gestapo or something."

Bert hung up and told the others what Jim had said.

Dave said, "I think we should still proceed with Plan A, but let's stop off and talk to Bill first."

They all got ready to leave. While Dave finished up the gift-wrapping, the twins went off to change clothes. They always tried to dress for the occasion, no matter what it might be. For example, when seeing a movie, they would dress according to the genre of the film. They wore gangster suits when seeing gangster movies, cowboy costumes when seeing westerns, and military uniforms when seeing war films. When eating out, they dressed according to the cuisine: kimonos for Japanese food, raincoats for seafood, and McDonalds uniforms when eating at McDonalds. However, they usually chose not to wear their birthday suits to birthday parties.

Tonight they decided to wear lab coats, and as part of the costume, they each carried a clipboard and kept a pencil stuck behind their ear.

While the twins were changing, Bert packed up the Icehouse set. They carried their set everywhere they went. This was one of the nicer sets—Icehouse sets ranged in quality from sets using cheap punch-out and fold-up cardboard pyramids (sold in dime stores) to extremely expensive, one-of-a-kind, polished stone pyramids (sold in jewelry stores). The most commonly used Icehouse sets featured translucent, ice-like playing pieces, made out of plastic. The Four's set was a little more exclusive, being made out of wood and painted in the traditional four colors (red, yellow, blue, and green). The sixty wooden pyramids fit neatly into a black leather pouch that Bert carried on his belt.

At seventeen minutes after eight, The Four exited their apartment and walked down the hall towards the elevator. When it arrived, they were disappointed to see that Doug was inside.

Doug was short and dumpy, with thick glasses and stringy black hair. He wore a ripped-up army jacket, and he seemed to spend most of his time riding the elevator, up and down. You might encounter him in the elevator on your way to work in the morning, and he would still be there when you returned that afternoon. All he ever seemed to do was ride the elevator, as if it were his home.

The Four got on. Dave leaned past Doug and pressed the button marked "1." As the elevator started moving, Doug said, "I went to New York a few days ago."

Everyone else in the elevator stared at the floor, trying to avoid looking even the tiniest bit interested in what Doug was saying. Despite the apathy of his audience, Doug continued. "I took the train. When I got there, I walked around the corner, and, um, I bought a soft pretzel. Then I came home."

At last the elevator stopped moving, but there was that usual delay in waiting for the doors to open. Days seemed to pass. Doug said, "Oh yeah, before I came home, I had enough money left to make a phone call, so I called my parents and told them where I was."

The doors finally opened, and The Four quickly exited. Dave, the last to leave, looked at Doug on his way out and said, "Good."

The Four strolled out of the lobby and into the warm night air of the City.

Chapter 3

On the west side of town, near the Geddes Point subway station, was a house that was commonly referred to as the Asylum. It was a small frame house in a more or less suburban area that was inhabited by a group of artistic souls who had banded together in order to ease the financial burden of Life. The inmates of the Asylum were: Jim, a writer; Bill, an inventor; Suzanne, an actress; Pauline, an artist; Torrence, a cartoonist; and Lynda, a musician.

The building had three floors: the ground floor, the upstairs, and the basement. Jim and Pauline each had rooms on the top floor, the third room there being a bathroom. The ground floor had five rooms: Living room, Kitchen, Bathroom, Lynda's room, and Suzanne's room.

The basement was given over almost entirely to Bill. Most of the space was taken up by his shop, which was cluttered with tools and various raw materials, to say nothing of a large number of incomplete inventions. In one corner was a furnished area, where he relaxed, and off from it were two finished rooms, a bathroom and a chamber little larger than a walk-in closet. The closet was where Bill kept his mattress, and at night he would lock himself in.

The basement bathroom contained the entrance to the last room of the house: the Bomb Shelter. You went in through a secret trapdoor in the floor, and this was where Torrence, the cartoonist, lived. He had managed to fix up the place so that it was quite functional as living quarters. The lead-lined concrete walls, fourteen inches thick, looked fine when covered with wood paneling, and the concrete floor was far less impersonal when covered with thick shag carpet. When he first moved in, Torrence found the place stocked with numerous cannisters of survival food, the "best used by" dates long expired and the containers themselves rusting. These he hauled off to an antique dealer, from whom, via bartering, he'd managed to obtain a large roll top desk. The installation of this, and a fairly shabby couch, into the Fallout Shelter was no easy feat, but once accomplished it made the room quite cozy.

Jim's room, on the top floor, was quite barren. The walls, which had once been a jolly shade of pink, had faded to a dull gray. Their adornments were few: a detailed map of the city and its subway, a color glossy photograph of Jim's parents, and a bulletin board to which was thumbtacked each and every rejection slip that Jim had ever received.

Jim did his writing inside a large walk-in closet. There he kept a desk, around which raged a hurricane of books and papers. When working, Jim would lock himself into his closet. When he had visitors, he kept the closet door shut.

Jim was a man who kept few possessions. His files, containing copies of all of the various things he had written, and his small library of precious books, were all that he truly valued. He was a man who kept his bags half-packed, who did not wish to be burdened by numerous material belongings. Several years of traveling had left their mark on him.

Pauline's room, on the other hand, was one of tremendous clutter. Each day, she brought home various objects that she had obtained, often by rummaging through other people's garbage. "You'd be amazed at what people throw away," she'd proclaim to anyone who seemed interested. The stuff she brought home fell into three basic categories: stuff she herself could use, such as old clothing and the like; stuff she could use as pieces of her sculpture; and stuff she could use as subjects in still life paintings. The room contained boxes and boxes of old things, plus a number of stretched canvases, some blank, some bearing partially completed paintings, and a number of constructions that Pauline liked to think of as sculptures.

Lynda and Suzanne each decorated their ground floor rooms with images that reflected their desired professions. Suzanne's walls were covered with movie posters, tacked up in layers that reflected her most recent genre interests. Since Lynda played the saxophone, her walls bore paintings and posters that featured saxophones. Her bed even had sheets that were decorated with numerous little saxophones.

The four private rooms above ground and the entrance to the basement all had separate-key deadbolt locks, which meant that anything beyond those five doors was considered open territory, a sort of no-man's land. It had become more or less a public place, open to everyone, like the lobby and hallways of an apartment building. The front door was never locked, and bore a small sign that said: "If you're cool, walk in." Because of this casual attitude, a great many people considered the Asylum a home away from home, and a hip place to hang out.

Chapter 4

None of the people who lived at the Asylum made enough money in their various creative endeavors to support themselves. Therefore, they collectively owned and operated a doughnut shop in a neighboring building. It was called "Dollars to Donuts."

The food at "Dollars to Donuts" was basic, and the menu very limited. They sold only a few things, but they prepared them very well. Their doughnuts were a dollar apiece, a bit steep for doughnuts, but customers paid this price willingly because the doughnuts were the best available anywhere. They were lighter and airier and tastier than any other doughnut sold in the City. On the other hand, their coffee was nothing special, so it was free.

The breakfast menu included sourdough pancakes of outstanding quality. The lunch menu featured an excellent Monte Cristo sandwich. And the specialty of the house, which was very often sold out, was chocolate angel food cake.

The restaurant itself was broken into two sections, like a gas station: full service and self service. In the center of the room was a large space filled up with tables and chairs. If you sat here, you placed your order at a counter at the back, and carried it to your table yourself.

Along either side of the room were a number of booths, and these tables received full waiter service. The booths were walled on three sides, and had large black curtains at either end of the fourth. When in use, the curtains could be drawn closed to allow the customers to eat and converse in privacy. These booths were very popular, and at peak hours, you might need to make a reservation in order to get one. Businessmen went there to discuss terms with clients, lovers went there to have arguments, and troubled people went there to be alone.

Chapter 5

At just about the time that The Four left their apartment, Bill began waiting on a woman named Denise.

Bill, the inventor who lived in the basement of the Asylum, was a strange individual. He had an odd habit of addressing everyone as "Norman." His middle name was Satan, and this at least explained his penchant for exclusively wearing bright red clothes. As an inventor he was something of a failure; though he had many ideas, he had yet to produce any invention that was both functional and marketable.

Denise sat down at one of the booths in "Dollars to Donuts," but she left the curtains open, not realizing that she could close them if she wished.

Bill trotted up to take her order. He immediately noticed that she was writing things down in a large black notebook. She ordered coffee and chocolate angel food cake, which just happened to be available.

A group of military officers came in and took another one of the booths, closing the curtains as they did so. Denise seemed particularly fascinated by this.

When Bill brought out Denise's order, he asked about her inquisitive nature.

"I'm writing a book," she said. "It's called *Great Diners of the City*. It will be a definitive guide to the area's diners, doughnut shops, coffee houses, and automats."

"That's nice," said Bill. "Everyone should have a hobby. Would you like to know what my hobby is?"

"Sure," said Denise.

"I build stuff. A couple of months ago, I built a nuclear warhead. Now, I'm working on a combination toaster/television set, which will toast bread with the radiation of the picture tube."

Denise forced a smile.

When she finished her cake, she departed. The entry in her book on "Dollars to Donuts" would eventually state: "Excellent food, fine atmosphere, but strange waiters. Four and a half stars."

Chapter 6

Six minutes after The Four left the lobby, three men came in looking for them. They wore long dark coats with the collars turned up and wide-brimmed hats pulled down low on their foreheads so that their faces were obscured by darkness. They were from the NRC.

The three men proceeded directly to the elevator. Doug was inside. As the men got on and pushed the button for the tenth floor, Doug studied them.

Doug said, "You guys cops?"

The leader of the men from the NRC said "No."

"FBI?"

"No."

"Gangsters?"

One of the other NRC men snickered. "No," said the leader.

"Then who are you?"

"None of your business."

The elevator stopped, and the doors slid open. When Doug found himself alone again, he said to himself, "I'll bet those guys were from the IRS."

Chapter 7

The three men found themselves in front of apartment 1017. The leader knocked. After a span of time, he knocked again. The door to 1017 stayed stubbornly closed.

However, the door to 1016, just across the hall, did open. A middle aged woman with graying hair and a blue apron beckoned to the three men. Seeing her signal, the men quickly ducked inside, and the woman closed the door behind them.

"If you're looking for those strange young men who live across the hall, you just missed them," said a balding man who appeared from elsewhere in the apartment.

"How do you know?" asked the leader.

"I watched them leave through the peephole," said the woman.

The leader tilted his head to one side and stared at the woman. "Do you always spy on them?" he asked.

"Oh, yes!" said the man. "They're a strange bunch. We keep an eye on them, for the sake of the community, you understand, in case we ever need to call the police or something."

"Are you boys from the CIA?" asked the woman.

The leader ignored the question. "What do you mean by strange?" he asked. "What sort of things do they do?"

"Well, there's all the usual stuff, you know, coming and going at all hours of the night, odd noises, weird people who come by..."

The two assistants were losing interest in this line of questioning, and began casually examining the features of the apartment. One of them noticed a large stack of National Enquirer newspapers and began thumbing through the top issue.

"I think they may be Russian spies," confided the man to the leader.

"I think they're either Devil worshipers or aliens from space here to plan for the invasion of Earth."

"They wear the strangest clothes. Once they went out wearing these black robes, with hoods down over their faces."

"And once I saw all four of them were dressed up like Elvis."

"And a couple of times they've gone out wearing animal skins and carrying clubs, like they were cavemen or something!"

The leader held up his hand. "Um—thanks for your time," he said. "But we've got to be going. Do you have any idea where they were headed?"

The man and the woman looked at each other. "Not really, no," said the man.

"Thanks, anyway."

Chapter 8

At five minutes after nine, The Four opened the door to the Asylum and walked in. In the kitchen, they found Pauline. She was sitting on a chair in the corner, eating. A cat perched on her shoulders, looking hungrily down at the food being eaten. The cat's name was Krypton, and it was one of six cats that lived at the Asylum. The cats were named for the rare gases; the other five were Argon, Neon, Radon, Xenon, and Helium.

"What are you eating?" said Bert with no small amazement.

"Communion wafers," answered Pauline. "I did this painting for a church down the street, but all they could pay me with was a big box of these things. Said they'd accidentally bought 500 boxes instead of 50."

Peter and Paul had their clipboards out, and they were taking notes. Peter listened intently to the conversation, writing down key things he heard, and Paul was walking all around the kitchen, opening up cupboards and cabinets, and writing down notes about his findings.

Pauline continued talking about the communion wafers. "They're pretty bland," she said, "But they're OK with Cheeze Whiz." She spread Cheeze Whiz onto one of the small, round wafers, and placed a second wafer on top of it, making a little communion-wafer-and-Cheeze-Whiz sandwich. "Want some?"

"Are you kidding?" asked Bert. "Isn't there anything else?"

"No one's filled up the refrigerator in a long time."

"But isn't it sacrilegious to make a meal out of communion wafers?" asked Dave.

"I don't know. Maybe. But I feel really good after eating them. They make me feel pure."

"Shouldn't you be drinking wine with those?"

"Probably, but all we have is Cranberry Juice Cocktail."

No one spoke then for several minutes. They all watched silently as Pauline made and consumed several more communion wafer sandwiches.

"Um, is Bill here?" said Dave.

"No, he's at work."

"How about Jim?"

"Yeah, I think he's upstairs."

They found Jim upstairs. He was sitting on the floor by the telephone. He was startled by The Four, and stood up quickly.

"Oh, hi guys, how's it going?" He seemed nervous, and quickly busied himself with picking up some dirty shirts that were on the floor.

"Hi, Jim." said Dave. "Did those three guys give you a hard time?"

"Um, no, it wasn't too bad." Jim's eyes were bloodshot and his face was dirty. He looked as if he'd been crying.

"What's wrong, Jim?" said Peter.

"Nothing. Look, um, I'll see you guys later, OK?"

"Yeah, all right," said Dave. "Take care of yourself, OK?"

"Sure," said Jim.

The Four went back downstairs, and then outside. "What's with Jim?" muttered Bert as they walked down the street.

Chapter 9

The middle-aged couple in the apartment across the hall from 1017 had just finished dinner and were sitting side by side on the couch. The television set droned away, its flickering blue light casting flickering blue shadows across the room. A small lamp with a green shade cast yellowish/greenish light onto the couple from an old wooden end table beside the couch. Pale moonlight shimmered in from the window.

It was ten minutes after nine. The woman said, "Well, shall we read the paper?"

Each week at this time the couple read the Weekly World News. They liked it much more than the National Enquirer, which they read two days earlier each week. The Enquirer spent much more time with articles about Hollywood stars and miracle diets. The Weekly World News, on the other hand, was given over almost entirely to important news stories, the news somehow overlooked by the larger, daily newspapers. The couple often wondered how a newspaper that came out every day and used up so much paper and weighed so much could ignore big news like the discovery of a crashed UFO on Mount Everest or the birth of a child with three heads. The couple had long ago stopped subscribing to the big newspapers, with their incomplete journalism.

Each week, when the Weekly World News was delivered to their doorstep, the couple would bring it in and leave it on the coffee table. They each carefully avoided reading the banner headlines or looking at the murky black and white photographs sometimes associated with them. The paper would sit on the table, unexamined and undisturbed, until well after dinner. They each savored the waiting, each concealing from the other their excitement at the prospect of soon reading this, their favorite newspaper. It was the high point of their week, and neither of them wanted to rush it.

And each week, they would sit on the couch, waiting until they could stand to wait no longer. Then, they would sit side by side, holding the paper between them, reading with amazement about the ghost of Bigfoot, the truth behind the Bermuda triangle mystery, proof of reincarnation, and the secret society that controls and manipulates the actions of top government officials everywhere.

"I guess we might as well," said the man as casually as he could, "there doesn't seem to be much of anything on television."

"OK," said the woman, trying to look disinterested as she retrieved the paper from its place on the coffee table.

The man and the woman looked at the front page of the paper.

The banner headline proclaimed:

RUSSIANS TEST NEW SECRET WEAPON

The man and the woman turned excitedly to the article, and began reading, their heartbeats racing, their breath quickening.

The article explained that the Russians had developed a way of increasing the radiation output from television sets so that it burned frequent television viewers to ashes.

The man and the woman gazed at each other in terror and astonishment. The man jumped up, dashed over to the television set, and turned it off. For good measure, he also pulled out the plug. Then he sat down next to his wife.

They sat there for a long time. Neither moved, neither spoke. They just stared at the blank screen of the television set, wondering.

Chapter 10

At 9:47, The Four took seats in a booth at "Dollars to Donuts," and pulled the curtains closed. While waiting for service, Bert brought out the Icehouse set, and they began a game. Bert was so angry about his defeat in the last game that he played with fierce concentration, aggressively moving against his opponents. He won in less than ten minutes.

Suddenly their waiter, who happened to be Bill, stuck his head through the curtains. "Good Evening," he said, "May I—Oh, it's you, Norman! How's it going, guys?"

"Hi, Bill!" said Peter.

"Did Jim tell you about the men who were here earlier?"

"Yes," said Dave.

"Well, I wouldn't worry too much about them. They seemed like a bunch of windbags to me."

"We're going to get rid of the, um, object in question anyway." Dave gestured at the gift-wrapped bomb that Bert had placed on the end of the table.

"Oh, that's it?"

"Yep."

"You could just give it to those guys, if you want, though I really can't imagine what they want it for."

"We already have a way of getting rid of it planned, don't you worry."

"OK. What can I get you guys?"

They all ordered coffee and doughnuts. Bert ordered two doughnuts, the others just one.

When the curtains were closed up again, Peter said, "What do you think, Dave? Could it be a real atomic bomb after all?"

"I could never have believed it before, but now... I'm just not sure."

"Who are those guys, anyway? And why are they looking for, um, That?"

"FBI, I suppose, or maybe Army Intelligence."

"Then it must be a real bomb!" said Paul.

"You know, I just can't figure it," said Peter. "Bill couldn't build an atomic bomb, not in a hundred years. He knows nothing about nuclear physics. In fact, when I suggested that he try it, he said he had no idea of how to go about it."

"Maybe he learned."

"And if it's a real atomic bomb, why has it taken so long for whoever's after it to look into the matter? It's been gathering dust in the apartment for months."

"You know how long it takes the Government to do anything these days."

"I guess. But how did they find out about it?"

"Whoever sold Bill the plutonium must have tipped them off."

"I still can't believe it's a real bomb."

"You want to push the big red button and find out?"

At that moment, Bill arrived with the food.

Chapter 11

At 10:57, The Four opened the curtains and emerged from their booth. Torrence, who was in the kitchen drying dishes, spotted them. He stopped what he was doing and went towards the front doors, arriving there just as The Four stepped through them and into the outside world.

"Hey guys," said Torrence, following them out, "I get off at one. Where are you going to be?"

"Hard to say," said Peter.

"We could be almost anywhere by then," said Bert.

"Our plans for the evening are still kind of up in the air," said Dave.

Torrence looked at his shoes. He wondered why The Four always gave him this sort of brush off. He wished he could find some way of being accepted by them. He liked hanging around with them, but they always acted like it was some sort of intrusion. He knew they liked him; he had seen how they treated people they truly did not like. For a while there had been this one guy staying at the Asylum, and The Four thought he was a real jerk. Whenever he was around, they ignored him completely, they looked right through him, spoke of him in the third person, and always acted as if he were not in the room at all.

"But they never act like that around me," thought Torrence, "so they must like me, at least a little bit."

Torrence wished that The Four weren't always so aloof. It seemed to him that they almost went out of their way to be distant.

Torrence said, "Well, maybe I'll run into you guys later."

The Four moved off toward the subway.

Paul lingered behind momentarily, and whispered to Torrence, "We'll probably be at the Cafe later on." Then he walked quickly off to join the others.

Torrence grinned happily as he went back in to work.

Chapter 12

After the initial shock had worn off, the man and the woman in apartment 1016 began trying to cope with their problem. They were faced with a difficult choice: either abandon the television set forever, or give up their faith in the printed word of the newspaper they so cherished. The newspaper provided great entertainment, but lasted only for an hour or two once a week. The television set was a constant and continual friend; to do without it seemed unthinkable.

"Umm..." the man said at last, "Do you really believe that about the Russians and their new Secret Weapon?"

"Umm... do you?" replied the woman.

"Well, it just seems strange to me that we never heard of it before," said the man. "Why didn't they say anything about it on the evening news?"

"Those news shows never talk about the important stuff," said the man's wife.

The man found himself thinking the unthinkable and saying the unspeakable. "Did you ever stop to think that maybe not everything that the Weekly World News prints is completely, well, you know, true? I mean, maybe they make mistakes from time to time..."

The woman was shocked to find herself agreeing with her husband. "Well, yes, I guess sometimes those stories are a little hard to believe."

"It just seems to me that SOME of the stories run by the Weekly World News would have to appear in other papers if they really were true. Remember that one story that said that the President was dead, but that he'd been replaced by a life-like android so that no one would find out? If that was really true, don't you think we'd have heard about it on the television as well? Once people found out about it, they'd have to promote the Vice President."

The woman chuckled. "And that story about the baby who could recite the Gettysburg Address on the day she was born? Who would ever really believe that!"

Soon the woman and the man were laughing up a storm at the silliness of the various far-fetched news stories they had once so fervently believed were truthful. After they'd calmed down a bit, the man said, "Well, should I turn the television set back on?"

"Sure!" said the woman, still snickering, eyes still moist from having laughed so hard.

The man plugged the set back in, and then paused, finger poised over the on/off switch. He looked at his wife. "Are you sure?" he said. They both gazed down at the newspaper, now lying rumpled on the floor.

"Yes," said the woman resolutely.

The man turned the television set back on, and sat down next to his wife on the couch.

Chapter 13

The Four got onto the subway again, this time headed for the Android Sisters' downtown apartment. The train rumbled and bumped and screeched through the dark tunnels.

Bert said, "Those doughnuts weren't enough. I'm still hungry." He stood up.

Peter said, "You going back to the dining car?"

Bert nodded.

Peter said, "Then get me a Coke." He handed Bert some money.

Bert went back toward the dining car. As he passed through the dual doors between the cars, he could smell the dank, musty air of the underground as it roared past him at 70 miles an hour. He had a long way to go, since the dining car was traditionally the last car of the subway.

Once there, he ordered a ham and cheese sandwich and two Cokes. He devoured the sandwich on the spot, and drank most of one of the drinks on the way back to the others. He gave the second Coke to Peter.

Chapter 14

The man and the woman had been watching television for about twenty minutes.

"Boy, it sure is hot in here," said the man, wiping sweat off of his brow. He looked at his wife, who was also sweating. "Yes, it is," she replied.

Then suddenly, without any other warning, the man burst into flames. His wife screamed once, then she too exploded in a ball of fire. Their bodies burned quickly; in under two minutes they were completely consumed, leaving only their shoes, and small piles of ashes on the scorched fabric of the couch.

The television set continued to bathe the room in glowing blue light. A man tried to sell toilet tissue to the two piles of ashes.

Chapter 15

At thirty one minutes after eleven, Bert knocked on a door on the fourth floor of a luxury apartment downtown. The door bore a large number, 412. Below it was a small metal plate containing a slip of paper on which was written, "The Android Sisters."

After a long pause, Dave said, "Try it again."

Bert knocked again.

There was another, even longer pause.

Dave pressed his ear up against the door. "I don't hear anything."

"Maybe they're at work," ventured Paul.

"Or if not, maybe someone there can tell us where they are," added Peter.

Bert said, "I'm getting sick of carrying this thing around. Here, it's your turn." He forcefully handed the gift-wrapped atomic bomb to Paul.

"Hey, be careful with that!" hissed Dave. "It is an atomic bomb, you know."

They all looked at the door to the apartment again, hoping it would suddenly open.

"Oh well," said Dave, "Let's try the Cafe."

Chapter 16

The Android Sisters were neither androids nor sisters, but everyone called them that anyway. Their names were Cindy, Wendy, and Mandy. Wendy was blonde, Mandy was brunette, and Cindy was a red head. They were all waitresses at the Saturn Cafe, and they were all very attractive and popular. They were the life of every party they attended, and they were very busy being the life of a party on the other side of town at just the time that The Four tried unsuccessfully to find them at their apartment. The Four couldn't have known this, of course, since they had not been invited to the party in question.

Chapter 17

At 12:57, The Four disembarked at the Iceland Street subway station, and began climbing the concrete steps to the surface. Suddenly, Paul froze in his tracks and let out a howl.

The others all stopped and looked at him.

"I left the bomb on the subway!" shouted Paul.

The others all turned away and groaned.

The Four dashed down the stairs and back onto the subway platform. Too late, the train was long gone.

Paul was agitated. "We've got to find that bomb!" he shouted. "If it falls into the wrong hands, the whole city could be destroyed!"

Expressions of alarm appeared on the faces of the various innocent bystanders who overheard this remark.

Dave held up his hand to calm the others. "All right, all right, just stay cool. We'll find it. We'd better split up. Bert, you and I will search the eastbound trains, Peter and Paul, you search the westbound ones. Meet back here at two AM."

The Four split up.

Chapter 18

At a few minutes after one in the morning, Torrence's shift at "Dollars to Donuts" ended. He changed out of the badly stained and somewhat soggy clothes he had worn on duty and put on a pair of white overalls.

The back door into "Dollars to Donuts" bore a sign that said "Employees Only" and faced on a dark alley. The door opened, and Torrence stepped out. He was immediately confronted by three men in long dark coats.

"Your name Torrence?" said one of the men.

Torrence wracked his brain for some clues as to who these men might be and why they were suddenly interrogating him. He found none. He could think of nothing he'd done wrong. He decided to play it honest.

"Yes," he said, trying to keep his voice from quavering.

"You know these men?" said the Interrogator, holding out a photograph.

Torrence took the photo and studied it. It was a picture of The Four. It was a very bad image, a fuzzy black-and-white deal. It was hard to make out who the picture was of, especially in the darkness of the alley. The photo looked like a copy made from film taken by a monitor camera in a subway tunnel. It was a very bad photo, but Torrence still recognized the subjects.

"Um, I guess I know them," he said.

"They were here tonight, right?"

"Yes."

"Any idea where they were headed?"

"Not really, no."

"Were they carrying anything unusual?"

Torrence thought for a moment. "Not that I can think of," he said.

"They didn't have an object with them, about this big?" The Interrogator held up his hands to show how big.

Torrence thought again. "Well, they did have a big package with them, but it was done up in gift-wrapping paper."

The Interrogator smiled. "Thanks for your help," he said.

During the Questioning, the Interrogator's two assistants drifted down the alleyway. One of them found a bent-up old monkey wrench on the ground, at which point a quiet argument ensued over which of the two had actually seen the wrench first. One of them pushed the other. The other pushed back. The one without the wrench tried to grab it out of the hand of his partner. They grappled, and rolled down onto the ground and into a couple of galvanized steel trash cans.

"Thanks for your help," said the Interrogator. Then he heard the crashing noise of trash cans being knocked over. "What's going on down there?" he hissed. He ran down the alley and broke up the fight. When he found out what they had been fighting over, he took the wrench and hurled it away into the darkness.

"Can't you guys behave for five minutes while I'm interrogating someone?" he shouted, as he led his underlings off down the street. "I'm gonna send you guys back to the office if you don't shape up!"

Torrence stood listening as the three dark-coated men moved off, until the sound of the leader's disciplinary voice faded away into the darkness. Then he strolled down the alley in the direction of the subway station.

Chapter 19

At 1:20 AM, a subway train screeched to a halt in the musty, dimly-lit tunnel of the Martinsburg station. The doors slid open, and Peter and Paul hopped on.

The car they entered was empty save for two people: a mother and her young son. The boy looked to be about seven years old, and was obviously very glum. As the train started moving again, he stared out of the window at the tunnel lights flashing past. The mother seemed exhausted. Though only about thirty, she seemed much older as she sat perfectly still in the bouncing subway car. She sat rather slumped, as if a 50 ton weight were perched upon her shoulders.

Peter said, "You go ahead and check out this train. Meet me back here."

Paul nodded and went off down the aisle.

Peter sat down on the bench across from the woman and her little boy. "Hey, kid," he said, "You wanna hear a joke?"

The mother stiffened slightly, but the boy's eyes brightened up and he spoke in a shrill voice: "Sure!"

"OK," said Peter, "This truck driver is hired to deliver a bunch of penguins to the zoo. So he picks up the penguins and puts them in his truck. He's told they have to be at the zoo by two o'clock.

"So he drives off down the road with these ten penguins in his truck. Unfortunately, a few miles away from the zoo, his engine conks out and he's forced to stop his truck on the side of the road. Now he's really worried, because he's afraid he won't be able to get the penguins to the zoo by two o'clock, which means he won't get paid.

"So he flags down another truck driver, and says to the second truck driver, 'Look, I'm supposed to take these penguins to the zoo, but my truck broke down. I'll give you fifty bucks to take them to the zoo for me.'

"The second truck driver agrees, they load the penguins into his truck, and off he goes. Then the first truck driver starts tinkering with his engine to see if he can fix it. After a while, he does.

"So the first truck driver gets back into his truck and drives off towards the zoo, to make sure that the penguins got delivered. But as he passes a movie theater, he is shocked to see the second truck driver standing at the box office, with all ten penguins lined up behind him.

"The first truck driver stops his truck and runs over to the second truck driver and the penguins. 'Hey,' he says, 'I thought I told you to take these penguins to the zoo!'

"'I did take them to the zoo,' says the second truck driver, 'But after that, I still had some money left over, so I decided to take them to the movies.' "

The little boy laughed, and his mother smiled. She rubbed his hair with her hand, and it seemed then that the buzzing fluorescent lights overhead were somehow warmer and brighter, that the weight on the woman's shoulders was not quite so heavy, that there was more in the world for the child to look at than the flashing lights in the subway tunnel.

Paul returned then, and Peter stood up. "Any luck?" he asked. Peter shook his head.

The train pulled in at the Frostdale station, and Peter and Paul got off.

Chapter 20

At 1:20 AM, a subway train screeched to a halt in the musty, dimly-lit tunnel of the Flaxelton subway station. The doors slid open. As Bert and Dave started to get into one car, they noticed a kid exit the next car down. He looked to be about thirteen years old, and was carrying a gift-wrapped atomic bomb.

"Look," said Dave.

Bert growled. The two guys stepped back away from the subway train, as it closed its doors and rumbled off into the darkness.

Bert and Dave walked briskly toward the kid, who was staggering slowly towards the "UP" staircase. The weight of the bomb was clearly a difficult burden for him to bear. Dave and Bert cornered him.

"Hey kid," hissed Bert, "Where'd you get that?"

"I found it on the subway."

"It happens to be ours," said Dave calmly.

"Get lost!" said the kid. "Finder's Keepers." He continued toward the stairs, trying to stagger a little bit faster.

"Challenge," said Dave, quietly, but with great authority. The kid froze. The word "challenge," spoken in this context, had evolved into a shorthand expression meaning, roughly, "I challenge you to a game of Icehouse, with high stakes on the line."

The kid turned slowly around. "You guys got a set?"

Bert nodded.

"This thing as the stakes if I lose?"

Bert and Dave both nodded.

"What if I win?"

Dave reached into his vest pocket, removed some money, and held it up for the kid to see. Three crisp bills, neatly folded, high denominations.

"Two against one ain't a fair game," said the kid.

"You against me," said Dave.

Bert removed two sets of pyramids from the leather pouch he carried and set them out on the grimy floor of the subway platform. The kid set the bomb down on the floor behind him, and he and Dave knelt down to play. A subway train roared into the station. As it rumbled out again a minute later, the game began.

Dave swung into action. His hand moved with amazing speed, tossing pyramids out onto the floor in seemingly random yet carefully planned patterns. The kid made a few meager plays, but the game was over just seconds after it had begun. The kid was Iced, and was too stunned to speak. It was a classic case of what can happen when professionals take advantage of gullible amateurs.

"Sorry, kid," said Dave, as he picked up the bomb and walked off toward the tracks. As Bert gathered up the pieces, another train screeched into the station, and Dave and Bert quickly boarded. Long after the sound of the subway had faded into the distance, the kid continued to sit on the platform, in silent amazement at the speed of his defeat.

Chapter 21

Torrence was riding the subway towards the Iceland street station, hoping to find The Four at the Saturn Cafe. The subway rumbled along, rocking back and forth, wheels screeching in the darkness.

The subway ground to a halt at the Flaxelton station. Torrence gazed numbly through the window at the underground waiting room. There he saw three people crouched down, doing something on the concrete floor.

Two people got off of the subway here, and one person, a tired looking old man, got on. The doors of the subway squeaked closed. At that instant, Torrence suddenly realized what it was he was looking at. Bert and Dave were playing Icehouse with some kid on the floor of the subway station.

Torrence jumped up with astonishment. He ran to the doors, shouting "Wait! Let me off!"

But by then it was too late. The subway was moving, and Torrence had a final glimpse of Bert and Dave as the train disappeared into the tunnel.

At the next stop, Torrence jumped off and caught another train, heading back towards Flaxelton. It took an agonizingly long time for the other train to arrive, and an even longer time for the train to get back to Flaxelton. At last it did.

Torrence jumped off of the train at the moment the doors opened. He was too late. Bert and Dave were gone.

Chapter 22

The twins stood on the subway platform of the Iceland Street station, waiting to be met there by Bert and Dave. They were bored. To pass the time, they began a survey of the structural integrity of the subway station. They walked about the tunnel, marking on their clipboards and discussing in serious and concerned tones the various facts which they observed. They noted and discussed cracks in the walls, and unevenness in the floors, and rust on the steel columns that supported the roof. They shook their heads slowly as they regarded the various degrees of deterioration in the structure. Peter discovered that he had a tape measure with him, so they spent a lot of time measuring cracks and marking down their sizes and locations.

All of this had a rather disturbing effect on the other people waiting in the station, and on the people who emerged from arriving trains. One got the impression from watching Peter and Paul that the whole tunnel was in imminent danger of collapse.

At 1:55 AM, Bert and Dave arrived, with the gift-wrapped bomb in tow. The Four climbed the stairs out of the subway and into the cool, dark night.

Chapter 23

The Four emerged from the subway tunnel at the intersection of 46th and Iceland, and walked briskly up the street toward the Cafe. Since it was now almost two AM, the streets were more or less quiet.

They stopped in front of a closed door set into a plain brick facade. Ordinary shops flanked the door on either side, a pawn shop to the left, antiques to the right, and at this hour, these other businesses were closed up, heavy steel gates protecting their openings, the owners at home, sleeping or watching television.

The door had only one feature: a small image of the planet Saturn, mounted at eye level in the center of the door. The Four stood before the opening and said nothing. They knew what was happening: they were being scanned. A tiny camera lens was concealed behind that image of Saturn. As the men approached, the man behind the camera pulled up their files to check their case histories, account status, coolness ratings, and so on.

A barely audible click indicated that the door was now unlocked, temporarily. Dave turned the knob, and in they went, glancing over their shoulders as they vanished from the street. The door closed behind them, and the lock snapped shut.

They walked down a darkened hallway, which made a right angle turn ten feet in. Here, a small sign lit by a blue light bulb said, "This Way." After another ten feet they came to a door, above which was a sign that said, "The Saturn Cafe." The door slid open as they approached.

The Cafe was busy, but not jam-packed; one would normally expect more of a crowd at this hour. Many of the Icehouse tables that dominated the center of the room were unoccupied, which was unusual considering the hours a person sometimes had to wait to get a seat at one of those tables. As The Four entered, the Synthesist in the pit began a new piece. The electronic tones poured out of the speakers and sailed up into the darkness of the ceiling, swirling in and around the various customers of the Cafe.

The lights were kept low in the Saturn Cafe. The designers of the interior had worked on the principle of "pools of light," that is, small areas of lightness here and there in the darkness. The room was generally quite dark, and there were no bright lights at all in the Cafe, only small, shaded lamps. Dim lamps were suspended over each of the tables, and small lights with blue bulbs protruded from the walls. The ceiling could not be discerned at all, since it was fairly high and there was no direct lighting cast upon it. The overall effect was like being underwater, an effect that the designers had deliberately cultivated. Special lighting equipment had been installed that projected faint streamers of light which danced across the walls, similar to those that reflect off of lighted swimming pools at night.

An attractive young waitress named Maria approached The Four. She was wearing a very small dress made of dark green velvet, with a bare midriff. On her head was the halo-like circle of aluminum that was worn by all of the Saturn Cafe waitresses. It was a grouping of rings, in all about two inches wide, which rested on her ears and balanced delicately across her forehead. It reminded one of the rings of Saturn, as it was clearly designed to, and it was the only thing that the waitresses were specifically required to wear, as far as uniforms were concerned. It was rumored that some of the waitresses wore nothing else, but this was rarely substantiated.

The Four ordered drinks, and sought out their usual Icehouse table, located at the back of the room, underneath the huge neon image of Saturn. Its rings were sculpted from blue, green, and purple tubes, the planet itself being formed out of yellow neon. They began a game.

Maria arrived with the drinks. These she placed into the circular holes at the four corners of the table. The drinks were served in laboratory glassware, 400 ml Pyrex beakers to be exact. This was the only size beverage served by the Cafe, since the tables had been designed to hold this particular form of tumbler. The design of the table allowed for a full playing area undisturbed by drinking glasses or other such mundane distractions.

31

A specialty of the Saturn Cafe was a sort of tea/chocolate combination, called ceetea (as in C-tea), short for chocolate tea. This drink was to tea what mocha is to coffee.

As Maria turned to go, Dave said "Are the Android Sisters around tonight?"

Maria said, "No, I think they're all off tonight, but I can check for you."

"Please."

Maria vanished into the darkness, and shortly returned. "Sorry."

"Thanks anyway."

Dave turned his full attention back to the game, and found, to his dismay, that he was in the Icehouse.

"Should have been paying more attention," said Paul.

Chapter 24

Unlike most clubs, which feature loud rock bands, the entertainment served up by the Saturn Cafe was exclusively instrumental electronic music. The proprietors had invested a huge amount of money in the Pit, stocking the sunken area of the floor with the very finest synthesizers and electronic keyboards that money could buy. The performer, called a synthesist, sat in this hole, surrounded by equipment. His music flowed forth from numerous speakers that were inconspicuously positioned everywhere in the room. Altogether, the Cafe employed several synthesists full-time, though you might hear only one or two of them in any given evening.

The synthesist currently performing had been doing a complex tune with a heavy rhythmic beat, but it had degenerated into a jazzy, futuristic jam-session. The synthesist had clearly stopped following his sheet music and was experimenting, trying out several variations of a certain lilting melody, making it all up as he went along.

Paul said, "So where do we go now?"

"I think," said Dave, "That we should try their apartment again. It was a hot day, and it's a warm night. They might have gone for a swim. Perhaps by the time we get there, they'll be home again."

The others nodded and grunted in agreement. They knew that from time to time the Android Sisters enjoyed sneaking into a neighboring apartment building's swimming pool for some quick skinny-dipping. It was easy enough to do... The Four had done so many times themselves. It was simply a matter of waiting until a sufficiently late hour and then climbing the fence. The pool was poorly lit at night, and the building's nightwatchman rarely ventured forth from his post at the lobby desk.

The Four got up, deposited some money on the table, and left.

Chapter 25

Maria stood in the kitchen of the Saturn Cafe, filling 400 ml beakers with ceetea, which was stored in gleaming chrome pots. She gazed through the porthole-like window of the kitchen door, out at the table around which The Four sat, out at Dave. She sighed.

She had gone to great lengths to be assigned to the waitress station that included the table at which The Four usually sat. She had managed to arrange her schedule so that she worked at the times they usually came in. Whenever she thought they might be there, she wore the most tantalizing and intriguing clothing that she could find. But Dave never seemed to notice her, except to ask her about the Android Sisters.

If she could just get him alone, she thought, away from those other guys, maybe she could get to know him better. Unfortunately, whenever she saw them, they were playing that stupid game. But what could she expect, she told herself, The Saturn Cafe was, among other things, a place for people to play Icehouse. What she really needed to do, she finally decided, was to find them somewhere other than the Cafe.

She looked out at their table again, and they were gone.

Chapter 26

The Four emerged from the Saturn Cafe. The night was much cooler now, the heat of the previous day all but forgotten. A cool breeze stirred the air, blowing the first fallen leaves of autumn up and down the quiet city streets. A woman rode rapidly past on a bicycle; except for her, no one else was about.

Almost.

The Four walked down Iceland Street towards the subway station. As they walked under a dim streetlight, Peter said quietly, "We're being followed."

The others glanced over their shoulders. Sure enough, three men in dark coats were walking briskly after them. One of the men said, "Excuse us, we'd like to ask you a few questions—"

The Four broke into a run. Down the street, down the stairs, onto the subway platform. The train had just arrived. "Hurry!" shouted Dave, "Move it!" The Four dashed through the doors and into the train, collapsing onto the benches to catch their breath. Bert, who had been the last to arrive, said "I think they made it into the last car."

"We'd better move forward then," said Paul. They passed through several nearly empty cars, and stopped at the car nearest the front. Bert kept watch at the little window in the door between cars.

At last the subway arrived at their destination: The Einstein Plaza station, five stops east of Iceland Street, on the blue line. When the subway doors opened, The Four dashed out and ran toward the exit. Fortunately, they saw no sign of their pursuers. They quickly headed southwest, toward the Android Sisters' apartment building.

Chapter 27

Maria ran to her boss.

"Mr. Bean, something's come up, can I have the rest of the night off?"

Mr. Bean scowled.

"It's important," Maria pleaded.

Mr. Bean looked over the situation. "Well, I suppose so," he said, "It's a slow night."

Maria put on her long black cloak, and headed for the door.

Chapter 28

Torrence approached the Saturn Cafe.

He had been there before, but always in the company of The Four. Now, as he stood at the door, waiting for the familiar click, he began to wonder if in the past he'd been let in simply because of who he had been with.

A full minute passed, and the door to the Cafe did not become unlocked.

Torrence realized that without The Four here to vouch for him, he was not going to be let in. As he strolled away he tried to comfort himself by thinking, "Maybe they're just not open."

When he was about twenty feet away, he heard the sound of the door opening. Turning around, he saw Maria slipping quickly outside. The door snapped shut, and she began walking briskly down the street, towards Torrence and the subway.

When she got closer, she realized that it was Torrence, the guy who sometimes showed up at the Cafe with The Four. She'd often felt sorry for him, as he sat there on the sidelines, almost participating in The Four's activities, but not quite.

As Maria recognized Torrence, so too did he recognize her. She was that gorgeous waitress who usually waited on him and The Four at the Cafe.

Almost at the same time, Torrence and Maria both said, "Have you seen The Four?" Then they both laughed.

Torrence said, "I kind of thought they were at the Cafe."

Maria said, "They were, but they left a few minutes ago."

"Any idea where they were headed?"

"They were looking for the Android Sisters."

Torrence frowned. He had a hard enough time getting The Four to let him hang out with them. The Android Sisters were even worse; they really gave him the proverbial cold shoulder. "Great," said Torrence.

"Yeah." Maria wondered to herself, "Why do they chase those girls around?"

A cat scampered across a darkened alleyway near them. Through a large steel steam grate in the sidewalk, they could hear the sound of the subway rumbling underneath them.

Torrence said, "You wanna go get some coffee or something?"

Chapter 29

At 3:13 in the morning, Torrence and Maria took seats at a booth in a diner on the north side of town. The Henderson Diner had once been a masterpiece of "Streamline Moderne" architecture, but over the years it had become pretty run down. Most of the Art Deco ornamentation had worn out or been stolen or broken by vandals. Everything had a sort of tarnished look to it, but the lights were bright, and the cheerful green neon, reading "Open 24 Hours," still shone in the window. Torrence told the old man behind the counter that they wanted two coffees.

Torrence and Maria sat looking across at each other. The silence was very awkward. Neither could think of anything to say. The coffee arrived, and they were able to clear the silence by concentrating intensely on the process of drinking the coffee.

After the coffee was all gone, however, the silence returned.

Torrence rummaged in his pocket and came up with a pencil. He began to doodle on the paper placemat. Sketching always eased his tension.

Maria took an immediate interest. "What are you drawing?"

"Oh, I'm just sketching." He drew a little picture of an ocean liner sinking.

"You draw pretty good," said Maria. She felt she had to say something.

Torrence brightened up. "I'm a cartoonist," he said. "I do a strip for a small magazine called *The Midnight Xerox*. Ever read it?"

Maria pursed her lips. "Sorry, no."

"Oh, well, it's a very small magazine, and it doesn't come out very often."

"I'll keep my eyes open for it."

Torrence drew a quick caricature of the old man behind the counter.

"Hey, that's great!" said Maria. This time she was actually impressed.

Torrence then looked right at Maria and began to sketch her.

"Hey, stop that!" she said. She turned her head to the side, and held her hand up in front of her face.

"Oh, come on!" said Torrence. "It won't hurt. Honestly, I'll never understand women. They spend hours and hours putting on makeup, shopping for just the right clothes, getting these wacky haircuts, all so they can look 'perfect.' But when you try to preserve that perfection, they raise a big fuss. I'll bet you hate having your picture taken, too."

"Yup."

"Why?"

"Because pictures of me always come out looking bad."

"Yeah, sure. Look, this one will come out good."

Maria rolled her eyes, but finally sat still and allowed Torrence to sketch her. The picture came out quite well, except that the circular stain on the placemat, caused by Torrence's coffee cup, ended up being a bit too close to Maria's shoulder. Maria smiled broadly as she studied the flattering portrait.

"You can have that if you'd like."

"Can I?" Maria was delighted.

"If you want, we could stop off at my place and I could show you some of my other artwork. I've filled up a lot of sketchbooks."

Maria gazed suspiciously into Torrence's innocent, honest eyes. "Where do you live?" she asked.

"In a bomb shelter," said Torrence.

Maria scowled skeptically.

Torrence became defensive. "It's true! Really!"

"All right," said Maria. "Let's go."

Chapter 30

Just as Torrence and Maria were leaving the Henderson Diner, Denise came in, intending to review it for her forthcoming book. She had just come from an Automat on 187th street, where she had greatly enjoyed a bowl of thick, creamy, chicken noodle soup. Now, she was interested in something for her sweet tooth, perhaps something chocolate, to top off the meals she'd had that day. Then it would be off to bed.

After some agonizing over the menu, she finally decided on and ordered a slice of chocolate cream pie.

"Sorry, miss, sold the last piece 'bout an hour ago."

Denise sighed, and settled on a chocolate milk shake. It came in a tall glass with a huge mound of whipped cream on top and a wafer cookie on the side. An authentic malt can containing an extra serving was also placed before her, and this attention to detail won for the diner the following rating in Denise's book, *Great Diners of the City*: "Beautiful architecture, although a bit run down, and outstanding desserts. Four stars."

Chapter 31

As Torrence and Maria entered the Asylum, they could hear the sound of Lynda's saxophone.

"There must not be anyone else here," said Torrence. "Lynda doesn't practice at this hour unless the house is empty."

"How many people live here?" asked Maria.

"Six people, and six cats."

Maria seemed interested in this, so Torrence gave her the grand tour. They strolled quietly through the empty house. Floorboards creaked. Several of the cats skittered away as they drifted from room to room. The mellow tones of Lynda's saxophone drifted along with them.

At three minutes after four in the morning, they climbed through the hatch and down the ladder to Torrence's room.

"Hey, this is really nice!" said Maria. "But it isn't really a bomb shelter, is it?"

"It sure is," said Torrence proudly. "The walls are made of reinforced concrete, fourteen inches thick, and lined inside and out with lead. I just put this wood paneling stuff up so that it would look nicer."

"What's all that stuff?" Maria indicated a large pile of cardboard boxes in the corner.

"Food and water supplies."

"Ugh! That stuff must be really old!"

"No, it's all fresh, I bought it just a few months ago. You see, when this shelter was originally built, it was stocked with food and supplies, but it was all stuff like cannisters of crackers. When I moved in, I got rid of it all, since it was unappetizing thirty years ago and inedible now.

"Then I figured, if I'm going to live in a bomb shelter, I might as well have a few supplies on hand. I mean, what if The Big War really comes? Wouldn't it be a bummer if I managed to survive down here but then didn't have any uncontaminated food on hand?"

"Yeah, I guess so, but..."

"So I went out and bought a bunch of freeze-dried stuff that will stay good for years, and a whole lot of bottled water."

Maria shrugged her shoulders. "Seems like a lot of trouble and expense to me."

Torrence looked down at the floor, and smiled a tight-lipped smile. "Well, I guess I just believe in being prepared. Besides, I don't have much else to spend my money on."

The sound of the saxophone floated down through the open trapdoor and into the shelter.

"You wanna look at my sketchbooks?"

"Ok."

They sat on the carpeted floor. Torrence held the books and turned the pages, and Maria looked on, occasionally saying things like "That one's nice," and "Oh, I like that one a lot." Then, Bill came home. They could hear him scuffling about in the basement above them. After a short while, he began pounding away at some sheet metal with a large hammer. The noise was awful, and drowned out Lynda's saxophone music.

Torrence got up, climbed the ladder, and sealed the trapdoor. The sound became almost inaudible.

"That's another nice thing about living down here," he said as he turned on a light. "You can block off the noise from upstairs."

Maria looked at him with sleepy eyes. "Come back over here," she commanded.

Chapter 32

At three minutes after four in the morning, The Four knocked again on the door to apartment 412, home of the Android Sisters. This time, after a short delay, Mandy opened the door.

"Oh, hi boys!" she said. "Come on in."

"Who is it?" came a shouted question from elsewhere in the apartment.

"It's The Four," Mandy shouted in reply.

There were some mumblings from the back rooms, giving The Four the impression that they weren't entirely welcome.

"Sorry it's so late," Dave apologized. "We were here earlier, but you weren't home."

"Oh, well, we were out. In fact, we just got back a few minutes ago."

"Oh."

Cindy and Wendy appeared from the back rooms. Cindy was

wearing a bathrobe and was drying her hair with a large yellow towel. Wendy said "What brings you boys over so late?"

Peter said eagerly, "We brought you a present!"

Bert, who had once again been carrying the gift, handed it to Mandy. "Oh, how nice!" she said. "What's the occasion?"

"No occasion," said Dave, "Just a surprise gift. Go on, open it!"

Mandy tore away the light blue wrapping paper. Her excitement faded as the paper fell to the floor. "What... is it?" she asked at last.

"It's an atomic bomb!" said Peter. "Bet you don't have one of those, do you!"

"Oh boy," said Cindy, "just what every household needs." She turned and headed back towards the bathroom.

"Well, that's really quite, uh, charming," said Wendy.

"I think it's very nice," said Mandy. "Thanks, guys. We will cherish it always."

At just that moment, there was a pounding on the door. "Open up in there!" said a gruff voice. Then the door burst open and the three men in dark coats charged in. One of them held up a badge.

"We're from the Nuclear Regulatory Commission," he said. "You are in direct violation of section 92 paragraph 43 of the Thompson/Lewis Atomic Weapons Act. You are under arrest for illegal possession, transportation, and concealment of an atomic bomb." As he spoke, his two associates cornered Mandy and attempted to wrestle the bomb from her. Being stronger than she looked, she put up a good fight, protesting loudly, "Get your hands off me! This thing was a gift! You can't just barge in here and take it from me like this!"

Suddenly there was a click, and everyone in the room froze. In the scuffle, one of the men from the NRC had leaned against the big red button and pressed it in. The various lights on the front panel of the bomb lit up. The big red digital counter underneath the words "SECONDS UNTIL DETONATION" suddenly displayed the number "60," which after a second changed to "59," then to "58."

Cindy broke the silence. "That thing isn't a real atomic bomb... is it?"

Now the men from the NRC swung into action. They produced tools, and began trying to take the steel box apart. The leader shouted, "We've got to disarm it, otherwise it will destroy the whole city!"

The seconds ticked away, as the three men desperately tried to remove the numerous bolts that held the box together. Progress was slow. "Boy, the guy who made this is a real nut," said one of the men. "Why'd he use so many bolts on this thing?"

The Four and the Android Sisters stood off to the side, holding their breath.

At ten seconds to detonation, it became clear that the men weren't going to make it. They frantically redoubled their efforts anyway.

The counter ticked off the final seconds. "3"... "2"... "1"... "0."

The counter stopped at zero.

Nothing happened.

The NRC men continued working away at the bolts, oblivious to the fact that the bomb hadn't done a darn thing.

At last they got the casing open. It was an empty box, with some electronics in the front panel and some lead bars bolted inside to give it weight.

For a long long time, no one said anything.

At last, the three men from the NRC turned to go. The leader said, "Sorry we disturbed you folks. Have a nice night."

A few minutes after they were gone, Dave said, "I guess it wasn't such a great gift after all."

"We'll get you something better at Christmas," said Paul.

Mandy smiled at them. "Thanks anyway, guys. It's the thought that counts, right?"

Chapter 33

"Hey, Bill! That atomic bomb you gave us didn't work!"

"Really?" said Bill, as he placed plates of sourdough pancakes in front of The Four. "Then I guess it's back to the drawing board."

"Tell me, Bill. Did you really think that thing was an atomic bomb?"

Bill leaned down, and spoke quietly. "Of course not, Norman. But I didn't think it would matter. Would you ever push the button on a REAL atomic bomb?"

The Four all laughed, and dug into their pancakes. The sunlight of the new morning warmed them through the plate glass windows of "Dollars to Donuts."

Chapter 34

A few hours later, at 11:20 AM, Jim staggered out of bed. He felt terrible. He had slept very badly. His head hurt, and his eyes seemed to itch.

He went into the bathroom to brush his teeth. As he did so, he thought back on the dream he'd been having just before he'd woken up. He'd already forgotten most of it, but he remembered a scene in which he'd been driving a station wagon through a city. Commercial establishments lined both sides of the street: restaurants, movie theaters, posh hotels, nightclubs, department stores, and so on. Everything had bright neon lights and big spotlit signs. But as he drove past these establishments, he realized that they were all false fronts, huge walls painted to look like buildings but which were really just fakes. The city was a fraud, like a movie set out in Hollywood. There weren't any real people there at all. And he'd driven on, out of the city and across an empty countryside. Eventually, he'd come to the ocean.

He forgot about the dream and thought about Jennifer. At first he failed to recall recent events, but then the news hit him again and he felt a wave of unhappiness flow over him. Perhaps it too had been a dream, he thought, wishfully.

He went back into his room and curled up into a ball on his bed. "I can't believe it," he said, over and over, to himself. "I just can't believe it."

He and Jennifer had gone out for two years, and now she had dumped him, for, it seemed to him, no reason. It had in fact been very sudden, though as he thought about it, he realized that she hadn't seemed particularly happy during the previous couple of months.

He stood up and walked around the room. He felt a strange tightness in his chest, like a hand pushing on his lungs. He found it very difficult to breathe, and worked hard at filling his lungs completely with air.

He decided to call Jennifer at work. She worked in a photocopying shop. He picked up the phone, dialed the first six digits of the number, and then hung up.

He curled up in his bed again and cried.

Chapter 35

In the evening, Jim had a shift at "Dollars to Donuts," and he worked his hours like a zombie, barely aware of his surroundings.

That night he had a dream. He dreamt that he was planning a party at his apartment, which was on one of the top floors of a very tall high rise apartment building. People were supposed to arrive at 8:00 PM, but they were all showing up at 4:15 in the afternoon. Jim wasn't ready at all. He hadn't bought any refreshments. His record albums were still in the bathtub. He was standing in the living room, surrounded by guests, who were whispering to each other about what a terrible host Jim was. At last he shouted for them all to leave, to go away, to come back later on, much later on. But they didn't hear him. He stood there, shouting, and they completely ignored him. He felt as if he were invisible, as if no sound was coming out of his mouth. So he ran away. He packed a suitcase full of doughnuts and ran away. He ran down the stairs and out to his car, only to find that it, too, was crowded with people who didn't seem to notice him. People were sitting in his car, leaning against the side, and sitting on the roof. A small child sat in the driver's seat, pretending to drive, whirling the wheel back and forth, honking the horn, shouting "Get out of the way! Move, you morons!" And suddenly Jim realized that he didn't even know these people, that they were all strangers. In shock and amazement, the suitcase fell from his hands and broke open on the pavement. Doughnuts rolled in every direction.

Jim awoke to the distant sound of an automobile collision. He heard the screeching of tires, the thud of impact, and finally, the soft tinkling of broken glass. He looked at the clock. It was 4:30 AM. Jim rolled over and went back to sleep.

And continued to dream.

He was sitting in a bus terminal, waiting for a Greyhound bus to take him across the country and back to his house. He was passing the time by watching television on one of several little black and white TV sets which were mounted on the armrests of certain chairs. He had to put a quarter into a slot in the chair every fifteen minutes, or the television would turn itself off. Jim had spent most of his money on the bus ticket, but still had a dollar's worth of quarters in his pocket.

Jim dropped a quarter into one of the television sets and started watching "The Jetsons." In the middle of the broadcast, there came a special bulletin. The television announcer said that a major and important garage sale was going on in Jim's home town. The announcer said that people were coming in from all over to pick up bargains at this wonderful yard sale. Reporters interviewed people on the air who'd bought great things at this rummage sale. The bulletin went on for a long time.

Then suddenly Jim realized that the yard sale was going on at his own house! In fact, all of the stuff being sold was his own stuff! He saw a picture of his mom, eagerly collecting money from customers. He watched as a fat old man paid ten dollars for his Silver Surfer sheets and pillowcases. Just then, the picture went blank and Jim had to put in another quarter.

He saw his mom selling off all of his most prized possessions. Jim stood up. He had to do something to stop this, he thought. He ran over to the bank of pay phones, but they were all in use. He ran back to the television, and saw his entire coin collection being sold for 35 cents. He screamed. He ran back to the phones. One had opened up, but when he put in his quarter and dialed, the phone was busy. He hung up the phone, but it didn't give his quarter back. With tears streaming down his face, he ran back to the television. It had turned itself off again. He shoved in his last quarter, and watched helplessly as everything that had ever mattered to him was sold off to complete strangers. Finally, the television went silent, but the sound of Jim's whimpering continued to echo through the huge, empty bus terminal.

Chapter 36

A few weeks fluttered past. One morning in late September, the Four stepped briskly onto a brown line subway train, headed for the Mayor's office. They had received an official summons and were dutifully reporting, as ordered.

The Mayor lived in a marble mansion downtown, in the heart of the City. This region, once a decrepit, ruined monument to the haphazard, random design of cities of the past, had been completely reborn under the Mayor's careful hand. The small, narrow streets and sad old buildings had all been swept clean away, and modern, well-planned, futuristic towers had been built to replace them.

The Mayor was immensely popular. He had been elected many years ago and had always been re-elected.

His Plan, undertaken early in his administration, was bold and innovative. One piece at a time, the entire downtown area was evacuated, demolished, and rebuilt. The small, worn-out old buildings and the tiny, narrow, traffic-clogged streets were all destroyed. In their place sprouted a true City of the Future: homes, offices, shops, government agencies, mass transportation, and public parks were all combined and intertwined in the new City.

You could take an elevator from your apartment in a towering condominium down to the subway, ride the train across town to your job, work in a sunny office, and return home via the supermarket, all without ever once stepping outside. The towering office and apartment buildings were linked together by a vast underground system of shops and subways. And when you did go outside, you entered a land of beautifully landscaped parks and lush gardens. No roads penetrated the downtown area at all, and in much of the outlying regions, cars were only permitted by special pass. Everyone relied completely on the complicated, comprehensive mass transit system.

Since trucks were not permitted in the downtown sector, an additional network of subways had been built to provide shipping of goods into and out of the center of the City. These "freight subways" rumbled back and forth, very deep below the surface of the earth, bringing cargo in from depots on the outskirts of the City that could be reached by truck. Large freight elevators brought the shipments up to the surface from the freight subway stations deep underground.

The freight subways did not overlap with the normal subways at all, and few people other than employees ever saw them. Everyone knew they existed, of course, and those who lived and worked downtown relied on the freight subways for everything—but they never saw them, which was just as well. The freight subways were darker, mustier, and far more utilitarian than the normal subways. The station's didn't even have names, they were simply numbered. However, the people who drove the freight subways did have names for the stations, names like "The Abyss," "Hell's Crossover," and "The Armpit."

The Mayor's mansion was the only building of the original downtown area to survive the Plan. It had originally been a library, with a marble facade resembling the ancient buildings of Greece and Rome. The insides had been gutted and remodeled to serve as the offices of the City government as well as the Mayor's private residence.

The Four had not been told why they were being called before the Mayor. Ever since the previous evening, when the courier had delivered the summons, they had been speculating about it.

"I just can't think of anything the Mayor could want with us," said Peter.

"Maybe it isn't the Mayor Himself," said Paul. "It could just be the Mayor's Office. That could be almost any branch of the City government."

"No, no," said Peter. "The thing said that the Mayor wanted to see us. Not So-and-so, in the Mayor's Office. It said 'The Mayor.'"

"Well, look," said Dave, "it obviously means one of two things. Either we did something wrong, and we're in trouble, or we did something good, and we're going to be thanked. The only question is, which one? Now, do you guys remember doing anything good?"

Silence fell upon the Four.

"Me neither. But it doesn't make sense that we'd be called before the Mayor if we were in trouble. We'd just be arrested, right? This is like going to the Principal's office in grade school. But it doesn't make sense. In real life, there is no Principal."

"Then it must be something good," ventured Bert. "Maybe he wants to give us the Key to the City."

"For what?" scoffed Dave. "What could we have done? It just doesn't make sense."

The others had no response to this, and so the conversation lapsed into silence. The Four leaned back against the subway train benches and let their minds wanders.

Bert looked at the other people on the train. It was relatively crowded, though not as jammed as it must have been an hour earlier. A woman across the isle from Bert was reading a newspaper, and the headline caught his eye. The paper was the Weekly World News, and Bert rolled his eyes when he read the headline:

ELDERLY COUPLE DIES OF SPONTANEOUS COMBUSTION WHILE WATCHING TELEVISION

At seven minutes before ten, the subway arrived at the Government Square station, and The Four disembarked. The escalators took them right to City Hall's main entrance. Their appointment was at ten, but it was a quarter after ten by the time they finished wading through the thick layers of security paperwork.

They sat in the outer lobby of the Mayor's office, each wearing an ID badge. Up until that point, they had been casual and unconcerned about the whole thing. But once they were actually sitting in the waiting room, they began to worry. They each fretted in silence, and the minutes dragged by. Finally, at 10:45, the door opened and an attractive blonde secretary said "The Mayor will see you now."

The Four filed silently into the Mayor's office and sat down in the row of chairs arranged before his desk. The Mayor sat reading some papers, and did not look up at the Four until almost a minute after they had gone in. He was bald, somewhat overweight, and quite old. But he nevertheless seemed friendly.

"Ah," he said, noticing the Four and standing up. He leaned forward over his big desk and shook each of their hands. "Hello."

The Four murmured various greetings. They were nervous, but they were also cool. Outwardly, they all seemed calm and relaxed.

The Mayor leaned back in his chair and folded his hands across his broad stomach. "No doubt you are wondering why I've asked you to come here."

Three of The Four murmured affirmative statements. Dave simply nodded slowly.

"Well," said the Mayor, "It's like this. Now that the Plan is finished, I'm finding myself with time on my hands. In fact, I'm even thinking of retiring. So, I'm getting back into some of my hobbies. And one thing I really enjoy is a good game of Icehouse. However, I'm not particularly good at it, and I could use a few pointers. So I asked my staff to locate some experts, and, well, here you are. Now... what do you say?"

The Four felt a little bit flattered and more than a little bit relieved. They made a show of modest refusal, but then agreed. The Mayor removed a wooden box from his desk drawer and dumped Icehouse pieces out of it and onto his desk blotter. It was a very nice set, carved from various exotic types of wood: Purple Heart, a wood with a natural purple color, Mexican Rosewood, which had an attractive striped pattern, and also Red Cedar and Ebony. He and the Four thus spent the next several hours playing Icehouse, right there on the Mayor's desk. Every few minutes, his phone would ring, and his secretary would say, "I'm sorry, but the Mayor is in conference." The Four taught the Mayor various strategies, and also showed him some exercises he could do to improve his skill at handling the little pyramids. At around one o'clock, they sent out for pizza, and the Mayor picked up the tab.

Chapter 37

Several weeks passed. Colored leaves fell and daylight hours shortened.

On a Friday evening in mid-October, Jim was sitting in a subway train, riding home. The daytime rush hour was just about over, and the nighttime rush hour was not yet underway, so the subway car was not crowded. Jim grew bored with the newspaper he'd been more or less reading and looked around him at the other subway passengers. One in particular caught his eye.

She was a very attractive young woman, with long red hair, hair dark and deep in color, a very rich shade of red. But it wasn't just her good looks that attracted his notice; she was wearing a jacket that struck him as being odd. It was a camouflage jacket, but instead of featuring blobs of varying shades of green, her jacket had red, pink, and purple colored blobs. It was like camouflage for use in the painted desert—or on the planet Mars.

Just as Jim was trying to think of a way to strike up a conversation with her, the subway screeched into the Zephyr Heights station, and she disembarked.

After the subway had begun moving again, Jim realized that the girl had inadvertently left something behind. He went over and retrieved a small red piece of paper from the molded plastic subway seat on which the girl had been sitting. It was a business card, which looked like this:

Meetings of
the Children of Mars
are held at 11:00 PM
every Friday night
in New Xi City.

Behind the words was a faint image of what appeared to be the planet Mars. Jim was immediately intrigued by this, and felt he had to find out more about it, partly out of curiosity about this group and what they did, and partly out of a desire to meet the attractive girl who had dropped the business card.

Chapter 38

When Jim got home he immediately began asking his housemates if they had ever heard of "The Children of Mars" or "New Xi City." However, only a couple of the Asylum inmates were at home.

Lynda was in the kitchen making a peanut butter and jelly sandwich. "Nope, never heard of either," she said, in answer to Jim's inquiries. "But did you ask Bill? Sounds like it might be his bag."

Bill was in the basement. Jim found him hammering pennies into larger, thinner disks of copper.

"What are you building?" asked Jim.

"New invention," grunted Bill between poundings of his hammer.

"What is it?" probed Jim.

"It's a secret," grunted Bill.

"Ever hear of a group called the Children of Mars?"

"No," grunted Bill.

Torrence was in the bomb shelter beneath the basement. He had closed the hatch due to Bill's hammering, but opened it to allow Jim in. Jim asked him about the Children of Mars.

"Sorry, Jim, it doesn't ring a bell. You might try asking The Four, though. They always seem to have their fingers on the pulse of the City."

Jim hurried up the street toward the Geddes Point subway station, hoping to meet The Four at the Saturn Cafe. Jim was really rushing now; it was already past nine, which gave him less than two hours in which to find out where New Xi City was and to travel there.

Chapter 39

Jim strolled briskly through the Saturn Cafe, toward the back where The Four were at a table beneath the large neon sculpture of Saturn. "Hi guys!" he said as he approached.

Peter, Paul, Dave, and Bert all kept their attention focused firmly on the table. They did murmur quiet greetings, but not one of them turned his head away from the Icehouse game in progress on the tabletop.

Jim pulled up a chair from another table and watched the game unfold. The tension beaded on the foreheads of the players and rolled down their faces as moves were made in rapid succession. It was the most intense game Jim had seen them play in quite a while.

As the game progressed, Jim became impatient. He was running out of time—it was now almost ten o'clock—and he had only a simple question to ask The Four. But they were so riveted to the game that he couldn't interrupt, and had to wait patiently for it to end. To pass the time, he ordered a beaker of C-tea, and leaned back in his chair, listening to the soothing music of the synthesist as it washed over him.

After almost twenty minutes, the game ended. Dave had won.

"Listen," said Jim, as Dave enthusiastically gloated over his victory, "have any of you ever heard of a group called the Children of Mars or a place called New Xi City?"

Peter, Paul, and Umberto quickly stated they had not; Dave, however, leaned back in his chair and muttered to himself, as if trying to recall an almost forgotten memory.

"Yes," he said at length. "Not the Children of Mars, but I have heard of New Xi City. It's a little sculpture park down by the river. It's on the purple line, I think, near the Riverside station."

"Great. Thanks," said Jim, as he paid for his C-tea and dashed out.

Chapter 40

Jim approached New Xi City with excitement and anticipation. It was just after 11 o'clock, and his quest was about to pay off. The night was clear and cloudless, with crisp, clean air and a sky hung heavily with stars. As he approached the little sculpture garden, he could see a number of people, standing in little groups, chatting and making small talk as if they were at a party.

The park itself was a small landscaped depression in the hillside, running right down to the edge of the water. All around the park were office buildings. Jim studied the sculptures. Five very large spheres of stone stood on the perimeter of the park, and a small fountain splashed quietly at the park's center. Jim could also see half a dozen or so other, smaller sculptures here and there in the park, but they were more abstract, and he had a hard time making out their details in the darkness.

The Children of Mars were gathered about the fountain. As Jim approached, he felt like an intruder, since many of the people there turned to look at him and their conversations momentarily lapsed. But after a few seconds, they turned away again and from then on mostly ignored him.

Three telescopes were set up near the fountain, and a small line of people waited to look through these devices. Jim could only assume that these telescopes were all aimed at Mars. Near this was a small table with a punchbowl and several trays of rather odd looking hors d'oeuvres.

Jim suddenly observed an important fact: everybody else he saw had red hair. He also suddenly noticed the woman he'd seen on the subway, who had dropped the piece of paper that had ultimately led him here. He made his way over to her.

"Hi," he said.

"Hello," said the girl.

"Listen, uh, I'm not sure I belong here, but I'd really like to know what this is all about," confided Jim. "Um... who are the Children of Mars?"

The girl sighed. "The Children of Mars are the descendants of the last survivors of the Martian race."

Jim rolled his eyes slightly and said, skeptically, "Oh, really?"

"Yes," said the girl. "A long time ago, we aren't exactly sure how long, the people of Mars were faced with extinction. You see, Mars was getting colder, and all of our water was locked in the polar ice caps. Our ancestors undertook vast engineering projects, building a complex system of canals to move the water down to our cities. But it was just too difficult. Our race was dying. Finally, they built a spaceship and the last few hundred Martians emigrated to Earth. Here, they mingled with the native human population and began a new life. Martians are physically very similar to humans, with one important difference: our hair, like our planet, is red. Red is not a natural human hair color. It is by this that we are able to identify our ancestry."

Jim's mind boggled at the girl's story. His basic instinct was to dismiss it as a silly idea that had started a small cult. But what if it were true?

"When humans and Martians began interbreeding, red hair became more common. But this caused a problem, in that the gene pool has become polluted. When you see someone with brownish-red hair or blondish-red hair, you are seeing the results of this. So, our group, the

Children of Mars, was organized to try to preserve our heritage and our genetics. It's mostly just a social group."

"And only people with red hair can join," said Jim.

The girl shrugged. "I'm afraid so. It's the only way we can confirm our ancestry."

"Well, thanks for the info," said Jim. He slowly strolled away, discouraged by the realization that, because of his dark brown hair, he didn't stand a chance of acceptance by either the attractive girl or the group as a whole.

As he wandered out of the park, he observed a small plaque near the entrance, reading:

NEW XI CITY
Hector Frizzz, sculptor
Dedicated to the memory of Xi City, Mars

On his way back home, Jim pulled the slightly-bent business card out of his pocket. He gazed at it thoughtfully, and when he got off the subway, he left it on the chair.

Chapter 41

On Sunday afternoon, The Four walked through the front door of the Asylum.

Peter and Paul went downstairs to the basement to talk to Bill.

Bert went into the kitchen.

Dave went upstairs to Jim's room.

"Hey," he said to Jim, "what happened on Friday night with the People From Mars?"

Jim was reclined on the floor near the window, reading. "Oh, not a lot," he said, looking up, "They're a bunch of—Hey! You have red hair!"

Dave looked at Jim blankly and then said "You have a fine grasp of the obvious. So what?"

"You're a Martian!"

"Huh?"

"You have red hair. That makes you a Martian."

"I see."

"This is what I was asking you about on Friday. There's this group of people called the Children of Mars, and they claim that people with red hair are descendants of the ancient race of people that used to live on Mars."

Dave made a sort of grunting noise, and smiled. "Well, that's pretty strange."

"Yeah."

For about 45 seconds, neither of them said anything. Jim closed his book and set it down. Dave stared out the window at the cool autumn afternoon. Wind stirred the trees, and colored leaves floated through the air.

"Hey, want to read my new story?" asked Jim.

"Sure," said Dave, with moderate enthusiasm.

Jim got up and went into his closet. After a moment he emerged with a typed manuscript, and handed it to Dave. The story was entitled, "The Empty City."

Chapter 42

Bert wandered downstairs, munching on a peanut butter and ham sandwich. He had used up the last of the bread in the Asylum to make it, a fact that he felt rather guilty about but which didn't keep him from thoroughly enjoying the sandwich.

Bill was showing the twins his new invention. It was a fairly large mechanical thing, constructed from all manner of old parts, notably including a variety of old clocks.

"What's that?" said Bert, through a mouthful of sandwich.

"Ah, Norman," said Bill, "You're just in time. I was just showing Norman here my new invention."

Paul looked at Bert's sandwich and said "What kind of sandwich is that?"

Bert said it was peanut butter and ham. Paul grimaced with disgust, and Bert tore a big bite out of the sandwich right in front of Paul's face, chewing it obnoxiously. "So," he said, again with his mouth full, "what's the invention?"

Bill leaned towards them, and, in a conspiratorial whisper, said "It's a Time Machine."

Peter, Paul and Bert all started yammering at once. "Does it really work? How'd you ever invent it? Can we use it?," that sort of thing.

Bill waved his hands to shut them up. "Well, I really should have said that it MIGHT be a Time Machine. I haven't tried it out yet. I think it will work—but I'm not entirely sure."

"Well, let's test it!"

Bill looked nervous, but also excited. "OK, you talked me into it," he announced, "I've been too afraid to try it up until now, but I guess I might as well."

He hunkered down and started fiddling with the thing. The device was composed of six wind up, analog clocks, of various sizes, bolted together and interconnected with many yards of gold wire. On the top was a gray steel box filled with electronics and covered with indicators, and also featuring a large green button marked "ENGAGE."

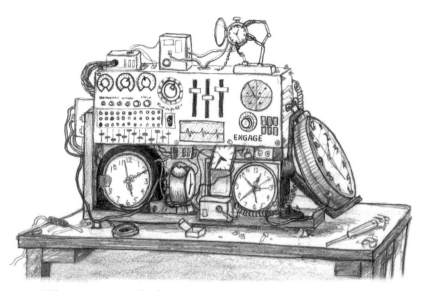

Bill was moving the hands on the various clocks, setting them to certain positions.

"I'm going to try to go forward to tomorrow. If this works, I'll come back with tomorrow's newspaper."

He stepped back and looked at the others and at his infernal machine. He took a deep breath. "Well," he said, "wish me luck!"

The others did so.

Bill reached out and grabbed onto the machine with his right hand, and pushed the green "ENGAGE" button with his left.

The machine made a buzzing sound, and there was a bright flash of light. However, Bill did not vanish away into the Future. He remained standing right were he was. A few wisps of smoke sailed up out of the machine, filling everyone's nostrils with a slightly charred smell.

Bert took a big bite of his banana and said "Guess it don't work."

Bill walked away from the device and sat down. "Another failure, I guess." Peter and Paul tried to comfort him. "Hang in there, you can't expect to get it right the first time! Keep trying! It'll work eventually!"

Bert finished off his banana and tossed the peel into the trash.

Bill looked at him. "Norman!" he shouted. "Was that a banana?"

"Yeah," he said, "but it was the last one."

"But weren't you eating a sandwich when you first came down here?"persisted Bill.

Bert said "No," with total authority. Food was always something that he was sure about.

Paul looked at Bill strangely. "It was a banana, Bill. I saw it." He paused. "Did your machine do something to you?"

Bill squinted his eyes. "I don't know. I was sure he'd been eating a sandwich before."

"But I'm sure I was eating a banana," said Bert. "I couldn't have had a sandwich—there's no bread."

Peter said "Come on, guys, we'd better go, Bill has work to do."

Paul said "Are you getting enough sleep, Bill?"

Bert said "OK, we'll see you later, Bill. Hope you can make your invention work—but I wouldn't bother calling the Patent Office just yet!" He laughed as they went up stairs.

Bill sat there thinking, wondering. He was sure Bert had been eating a sandwich. It was as if something had shifted when he tested the machine. But how?

Chapter 43

"THE EMPTY CITY"
By James L. Ruckel

One evening in late August I returned home to find a cardboard box sitting in front of the door to my apartment. It contained nothing of importance—a few books, some records, a sweater. I stored them in my closet.

Not long after that, I found myself unable to sleep. Each night, I would return from my place of employment, eat a T.V. dinner, and then, if I were lucky, I could take a nap. An hour, maybe two. But after that I was wide awake, and nothing I did could bring sleep to my eyes. I would wait under the covers, looking at the ceiling, until dawn stabbed through the curtains.

I tried all the usual things: I washed handfuls of sleeping pills down with warm milk. I read enormous volumes of great literature, and I listened to Frank Sinatra on the radio. I bought a record of the sound of the ocean. I went to a doctor who tried hypnosis and taught me various relaxation techniques. But nothing helped. I could not sleep. After awhile, I gave up trying.

By October of that year, I had become used to my insomnia, and I settled into a regular routine. After my nap, I would turn on the T.V. and watch late night programming until about 3:00 AM, when most of it ends. Then, I would wrap myself up in blankets and skulk about the apartment, working on little projects, until the sun came up. I solved ten thousand piece puzzles, I wrote to newspaper advice columnists, I sewed up the holes in my socks.

Winter arrived. I had to bundle up with more blankets as it got colder, because my landlord had a habit of pretending that the heating system was broken, in order to save on utilities. On particularly cold and snowy nights, I stayed in the kitchen and cooked up instant cakes and ready-to-bake cookies. I usually did not eat them, but the heat of the oven was a comfort.

In the spring, I came to the conclusion that my inability to sleep was due to some sort of deficiency in my life; I felt that something important was missing, but I didn't know exactly what. Therefore, I decided to effect changes. I got a haircut, and started growing a beard. I wore different styles of clothing. I moved into the city. But my life proceeded much as it had before, and sleep remained impossible.

My new apartment was on the fourteenth floor of a gleaming new residential complex. Living downtown was expensive, but I was able to afford it, having little else to spend my money on. The city was crowded during the day, but at night it was surprisingly empty. It seemed that everyone came to work in the city by day, but went home to the suburbs at night. My whole apartment building seemed to have only half a dozen residents. I sometimes wondered if all of the skyscrapers were even real buildings. I imagined them to be great hulking machines, quietly performing some unknown task.

On the warm evenings of summer, I took to strolling through the empty streets. It was very calm and pleasant. I felt quite comfortable, alone with the huge gray slabs of concrete and the quietly winking neon signs. But I soon realized that I wasn't completely alone. There were others like me in the empty city. I saw them in alleyways and on street corners. They sat alone in all night coffee shops. A few sat on benches in bus terminals. But most of them sat alone at the windows of darkened rooms, ducking out of sight when I happened to gaze in their direction.

I saw them often, but never spoke to them. We all knew there was nothing to say. I did look into their eyes, and I could see they were all waiting for something. As I was.

The summer slowly passed. One night, my wanderings took me to an old warehouse. I went in, and was met with a voice:

"What are you doing here?"

"I'm sorry," I replied, "I thought this place was empty."

"You didn't answer the question."

"Um...I'm looking for something."

"What?"

"I'm not sure."

"Is it something you lost?"

"Something I never really had."

"Then how do you know you want it?"

I gave no answer.

"Well," said the voice in the darkness, "I hope you find it."

"So do I," I said, as I turned and left.

One evening it rained, and I managed to sleep for over three hours. And I had this dream:

I was seated at a table in a very expensive restaurant. There were no menus. The waiter brought me a thick, juicy steak. I took up knife and fork, and sliced off a large bite. I chewed slowly. It was the most succulent and delicious taste I could imagine. My heart leapt at the new flavor. I prepared to swallow. Then arms seized me, hands gripped me by chin and forehead, and my mouth was forced open. Large metal tongs were brought forth. The bite of meat was removed and discarded. I watched helplessly as my steak was served to another man. Then I was lifted from my chair, and thrown out into the street.

I had gained favor with my boss by taking on the unwanted night shift... it was easy enough for me, since I was up all night anyway. But the strain was wearing me down, and the quality of my work was slipping. Eventually, my boss took notice. One day, called me into his office to talk to me about it.

"I don't want to be hard on you," he said. "You've been such a good employee for so long."

I nodded in agreement.

"But you must realize my position. If the work is done poorly, I have to answer for it."

I nodded. He held up a small plastic part, the manufacture of which I was responsible for. It was called Part Number 37. It would eventually be used in the assembly of electric can openers.

"Now look at this 37," said my boss. I looked at it. It was misshapen and discolored. "We can't use a damaged part like this."

I nodded.

"A factory runs on teamwork. You know that. Yet your fellow workers say that you have been acting strangely towards them."

"I haven't been sleeping too well of late."

"I see. Well, I'm not going to give you an Official Reprimand this time, but see to it that your work improves."

"Yes sir." I turned to go.

"Have you tried sleeping pills?"

"Yes. They don't work. That's not what I need."

As fall enveloped the city, and the nights began to get nippy, I started to frequent a particular doughnut shop. I enjoyed its pleasant atmosphere. It was warm and bright inside, and the strong smell of doughnuts was intoxicating. For most of the night, a round woman named Beatrice ran the shop. I knew her name was Beatrice because she wore a little plastic badge engraved with the name Beatrice. She was perfect for the job. She had a smile permanently tattooed onto her face, and phrases like "have a nice day" and "thank you come again" rolled off her tongue without any apparent effort on her part. When no customers required her attention, she would sit down behind the counter and read romance novels.

Around 4:00 AM, a friendly old man named Peter would emerge from the cold gray city, and begin cooking the doughnuts for the coming day. He had the strange habit of whistling the theme music from various T.V. shows as he pounded the dough and formed it into doughnut shapes.

At about 6:00 AM, a quiet young woman named Sally came in to take over for Beatrice. Sally had glasses, and long brown hair which she usually kept up in a bun. For two weeks I sat waiting all night for her to arrive; when she did, I unobtrusively watched her every movement until almost 8:00 AM when I had to go to the factory.

Then one morning, she spoke to me.

"What's your name?"

The sound of her voice made me jump. "William," I said," What's yours?"

"Sandra."

"Then how come it says Sally on your badge?"

"They didn't have any Sandra nametags so they gave me the closest thing they had."

"Oh."

"So what brings you into this place every night?"

"I can't sleep."

"Not at all?"

"Well, sometimes for an hour or two."

"Have you tried..."

"I've tried everything."

"...bedtime stories?"

"Um...no."

"When I was a little girl and couldn't get to sleep, my mother read me bedtime stories. Worked every time."

She took a paper bag out from under the counter and wrote her phone number just above the words "Fresh Delicious Doughnuts." "Here. Call me up tonight, and I'll read you a bedtime story."

"Thank you."

As I walked to the factory that morning, I found myself yawning.

Chapter 44

Dave handed the manuscript back to Jim. "Well?" asked Jim.

"It's interesting," said Dave, "that's for sure. But... well, I'm not certain that I really understand it."

"Hmm." Jim flipped through the manuscript. "I wanted it to be sort of odd and mysterious, but I may have been too subtle. Did you understand the stuff at the beginning?"

"Where the guy finds the box of stuff on his doorstop? No, not really."

"Yeah, no one else has either. I figured that would be a fairly obvious clue, but I guess it isn't."

"What is it?"

"Well... who do you think owned the stuff in the box?"

"Um, the main character?"

"Right. And who put the box on his doorstep?"

"Hmm. I don't know."

"Well, it wasn't the main character, even though the stuff in the box belonged to him. Who else might have had it?"

Dave scratched his head. "I don't know. A friend of his, I guess."

"Close. It was his girlfriend. See, at the beginning of the story, the main character is dumped by his girlfriend. I symbolized this by having him find the things he had loaned to her during the relationship returned to him in a very summary fashion. He puts the stuff into a closet and tries to forget about it, because he doesn't want to deal with it."

"That makes sense, but I didn't realize that when I read it."

"Well, I wanted it be subtle. I figured that by the end, people would have understood it, or at least understood what the story was about."

"Hmm. What is the story about?"

"It's about loneliness. At the beginning of the story he gets dumped, and then during the story we see how being alone affects him. He can't sleep, he wanders the streets alone, his work suffers, and so on. Finally, at the end, he meets somebody, and it shows signs of turning his life around."

Dave nodded.

"And the Empty City," continued Jim, "is my metaphor for being alone. When you're alone, romantically and unwillingly that is, you live in the Empty City." Jim sighed. "Which is where I live now."

Dave smiled a half smile. "Yeah. Well, it's a cool story anyway."

Voices echoed in the stairwell. Bert, Peter, and Paul were coming upstairs. They were arguing loudly about Bill's invention.

"All I know," said Paul, "is that it would be really cool if Bill really invented a working Time Machine."

"Hey Dave," said Peter, "Let's go."

"Where are you guys going?" asked Jim.

"Saturn Cafe. You want to come along?"

"No, I guess not. I'll see you guys later."

Chapter 45

Several days passed.

"Well, what do you think?" asked Pauline.

"Um... I like it," said Torrence. "But what is it?"

They were discussing Pauline's latest sculpture. She had brought it down from her studio/bedroom on the Asylum's top floor and set it on the kitchen table so that anyone around could easily inspect it and offer opinions. Torrence was unfortunate enough to have been in the kitchen cooking himself an omelet when Pauline barged in with her sculpture.

The sculpture itself was about six inches tall, and was basically a squat, three sided pyramid. It seemed to be made of badly tarnished silver. Near the top, a round hole went through the pyramid, diagonally entering one face and exiting another. Near the bottom, several metal tubes projected out from various points and angles.

"What kind of omelet is that?" asked Pauline.

"Bacon and chive," said Torrence. "Do you want some?" he offered, with obvious reluctance.

"No, I guess not."

"Good. What's the sculpture for?"

"It's something I'm doing for the Children of Mars."

"Oh really? And who are the Children of Mars? A few weeks ago, Jim was asking anybody who'd listen if they knew who the Children of Mars were. I don't know if he ever found out."

"He should have asked me," said Pauline. "I've known about them for a long time. The Children of Mars is this obscure group, I don't know if you'd call them a religious cult or just a club or what. They believe that many years ago an advanced civilization existed on Mars, and that when it fell apart, the last survivors migrated to Earth to survive. Supposedly Martians all had red hair, and Humans never did, until the two races started interbreeding."

A smirk was developing on Torrence's face as he listened to this. "Are you a member of this group?"

"Well, it's a real loose organization. They have weekly meetings, but they're really just parties. The policy is that anyone who has red hair is automatically a member. As for me, they said my 'heritage' is sort of questionable, since my hair is really strawberry blond, not red, but they let me in anyway."

"OK, but what exactly does this group do?"

"I think at first it was just a social thing, a way for redheads to meet other redheads. In fact for a long time I think it was meant to be a secret organization. But lately they've been trying to get more exposure. I think they want people to believe their claim of a once-great Martian civilization."

A radio blared quietly on the other side of the kitchen table. It was tuned to a top 40s station, which was currently broadcasting a song called "Bombs in the Gutter" by the group World War 4. Torrence had been finding this tune increasingly annoying. He finally reached over and snapped the radio off.

"Do you believe in a once-great Martian civilization?" asked Torrence.

"Well, I didn't use to, but now I'm not so sure."

Torrence shoveled the last bite of his omelet into his mouth.

"You see, the big claim they make, or rather that the Emperor makes—"

"The Emperor?"

"Yeah, his name is Hector Frizzz, he's more or less the leader of the group. They call him 'The Emperor of Mars.' Anyway, his big claim is that anyone who has red hair is a descendant of the Martians, and therefore has ancient Martian memories stored in his subconscious. Since this is a 'race memory,' it has to be considered as a whole. Anything that any given Martian descendant might remember would mean little on its own, since it would be just a tiny piece of a big puzzle. But if everyone puts everything they remember together, it might just add up."

By this time, Torrence was practically laughing out loud.

"Look," Pauline protested, "I'm just telling you what they believe, I'm not saying I believe any of this!"

"It's still funny!" laughed Torrence.

"But at times it seems like there might almost be something to it. The idea is that the subconscious Martian memories can be brought to the surface through creative work, so that when, for example, a redheaded painter paints something abstract, thinking he's just creating new images, he's actually tapping into his subconscious Martian race memories, and is painting a scene from life on Mars.

"The payoff to this theory comes when you look collectively at the creative works of a number of different red haired artists. Their works, while differing in style, method, and medium, still have strikingly similar themes and elements. And my sculpture does fit into this category."

ANDREW LOONEY

Torrence had stopped laughing and was listening rather more intently now.

"The best example of this is Icehouse. Have you heard the recent commercials for the game that call it 'The 100,000 Year Old Game from Mars?' That's not just an advertising gimmick, the guy who invented it really believes that."

"Who invented it?"

"I'll give you one guess." She paused, but Torrence just shrugged. "The Emperor of Mars! Of course, he claims that when he figured out the rules and stuff he was really just tapping into the Martian race memory. In fact, I think he says he got the original idea for the game from a dream he kept having."

"Yeah, but—"

"But he could have just made the whole thing up, right? So what! The concept is that even if you think you are creating something out of the blue, it could really be subconscious memories you are tapping into as part of the creative process. Even if he secretly thinks he made the whole shtick up, it could still be true."

"OK, OK," said Torrence, "then what is this thing supposed to be?" He picked up her new sculpture and rotated it around in his hands, looking at it from all angles.

"Well, I don't really know. Maybe it's a copy of a sculpture originally done on Mars, or maybe it's a non-working replica of some common Martian object, like a Martian toaster, perhaps. But probably, this whole Martian angle is just a load of crap, and this is just a dumb abstract sculpture thrown together one afternoon by a not very good Human artist."

"Don't be so hard on yourself," said Torrence. "I think it's kind of neat. What do you call it?"

"I haven't given it a title yet."

"Then I think you should call it 'Martian Toaster.' "

Pauline shrugged her shoulders, took her sculpture back from Torrence, and carried it upstairs to her room.

Chapter 46

Bill considered the problem of his non-functional time machine for several days. After the first test failed, he had almost completely dismantled the device, searching for mistakes, incorrectly connected wires, flaws in his design, and anything else that could have kept it from working properly. But everything seemed correct.

So he'd put it back together and tested it again. Again there was a flash and a lingering burnt smell, and again he completely failed to float off into the future.

For an hour or so, he'd puttered about with the machine, attempting to figure out if it had done anything at all, eventually concluding that it hadn't. In frustration, he'd gone upstairs to find something to eat.

And there, he discovered another clue.

For several months, Suzanne and Lynda had been talking about painting the kitchen. They both agreed it needed it desperately, though they were unable to see eye to eye on what color it should be. Suzanne favored white, Lynda wanted yellow. And in the last few days, they'd decided to stop talking about it and actually do it. And that very morning, just as Bill had finished making his coffee, they'd barged in with brushes and dropclothes and had started painting the kitchen white.

When Bill wandered upstairs to find a bit of lunch, he was shocked and amazed to find them painting the kitchen yellow.

"I thought you were going to paint this white," Bill asked the girls in astonishment.

Suzanne answered him. "We tossed a coin, and she won."

Forgetting his hunger, Bill ran back downstairs.

He'd been sure that Bert had been eating a sandwich, not a banana, despite the physical evidence to the contrary. Now he found his housemates painting a room yellow when they'd previously been painting it white.

He looked at his machine. Suddenly he understood.

"This isn't a Time Machine," he said, "It's a Time Shifter!"

Through some mistake in his logic, he had made a machine that somehow changed the past. It actually seemed to alter time slightly, to make minor changes in history. It was a machine that "shifted" the recent past, a Time Shifter.

Bill thought about the implications of this. He seemed to have no control over what changed. It seemed to be entirely random. First a sandwich changed to a banana, then a decision about paint color was altered, based entirely upon the way a coin had fallen.

What would change the next time he pushed the button? The changes he'd seen so far had been of no real significance... but what if the next change resulted in someone's death? He also had no idea of how far back in time the Time Shifter could effect changes; perhaps the next time he pushed the button, he'd find himself in a world where the Nazis had won World War II.

Furthermore, only he seemed able to remember the previous incarnation of things. Everyone else was totally unaware of the changes in history. Perhaps being in contact with the Time Shifter somehow had an umbrella effect on him, making him the only person with intact memories of the way things had been before.

He worried greatly about what to do next. Should he destroy the machine now, before something dreadful happened, or instead continue with his experimentation?

Chapter 47

On a Friday night early in November, The Four walked into the Saturn Cafe. With them was Jim. On their way in Jim snagged a copy of the City Paper, a free weekly newspaper that catered to the hip (and the would-be hip), large piles of which were deposited in front of the Cafe and a thousand other drop points in the City every Thursday afternoon.

They went to The Four's usual table, and The Four set up for a game of Icehouse. Jim pulled up an extra chair near their table and started reading his City Paper. Mandy, one of the Android Sisters, appeared and took their order. Five C-teas and a plate of Tringos. Tringos were triangular chocolate sandwich cookies similar to Oreos but with a lighter, less bitter chocolate.

In addition to her Saturn headpiece, Mandy was wearing a tight fitting gown with a severely asymmetrical skirt. The left side of her gown was a full length dress, sweeping down from her hips to drag on the ground, but the right side was very short, virtually a mini-skirt. The gown had a very dramatic diagonal cut and exposed her right leg quite attractively. The neckline was similarly asymmetrical, low cut only on the left side of the bodice. The fabric was a metallic gold material which shimmered when she moved.

Cindy and Wendy were also working at the Cafe that night, and when they drifted in it turned out that they were wearing gowns identical to Mandy's except in color, Cindy's being silver and Wendy's the color of copper.

While The Four went to war at the Icehouse table, Jim read his paper. He perused the Personals carefully, but found none worth responding to. The majority were placed by Single White Males, and the few he saw from Single White Females sounded either fat or boring or both.

At 37 minutes after 9 PM, a group of people entered the Cafe. Jim noticed them immediately because among them was the beautiful red haired woman with the red camouflage jacket he had seen on the subway and followed to New Xi City. The group included several other redheads.

"Hey Dave," whispered Jim, "when you get a chance, check out the people who just came in. They're from Mars."

Dave nodded, and when he got to a point in the game where he felt he could divert his attention, he looked at the group Jim indicated.

They were five, three men and two women, four of whom were Martians. They were seated at a table near The Four, and were starting a game of Icehouse. Each of the players had carried his pyramids in a special case and withdrew them with extreme care.

One person's set
was made of polished black onyx, and
he carried it in a long wooden case lined with velvet.
Another player's set was made of crystal, and the third, one of the
women, had a set made of silver with intricately carved scrollwork
inlaid with gold leaf. The fourth player's set was as noticeable as the
others, not for its elegance but for its crudity. He was an older man
who was balding, and the hair he did have left was of a very rich red.
His set was made of rough plaster of paris. It was lumpy, painted with
glossy red paint, and had obviously seen a lot of use. The woman with
the camo jacket wasn't playing, but sat near him, watching the game
with detached interest.

When Dave had finished playing all of his pieces, he announced
that his pad was clear and left the table. This was risky, since the game
was not over and with his attention removed, the other three could
gang up on him and possibly put him in the Icehouse, but Dave was
confident in his position and more interested in other things anyway.

He wandered over to the Martians' table to watch them play. They
were good, and Dave was impressed. Dave was also impressed by the
long haired Martian in the camo jacket, and smiled broadly at her. She
smiled back, and said "Hi there," in a warm quiet voice.

"Hello," replied Dave. "Your friends are good."

"Mmm, yes, they are," she said, and then laughed.

Dave smiled, and then said "What's so funny?"

"Nothing," said the woman.

The balding man hissed irritably at Dave and the woman, though
he didn't look away from the playing field. Then he played a couple of
his tired looking plaster pyramids.

The woman stood up and silently walked off. Dave followed her,
and they sat down at a table near the synthesist's pit.

"Sorry," she said, "They don't like noise when they play."

"I understand completely."

Suddenly the woman reached up, grabbed a tuft of Dave's red hair, and tugged on it gently. "This isn't fake, is it?" she said, smiling.

Dave sat back, startled both by the question and the fact that she touched him. "What?" he said in surprise.

"The color I mean. You haven't been dying this hair, have you?"

"No, of course not, why would I do that?"

"People have their reasons."

Dave shook his head slowly in confusion.

The woman stuck out her hand. "My name is Christina," she said as they shook hands, "but most people call me The Martian Princess."

"Pleased to meet you. I'm Dave."

"Hi."

There was a moment of awkward silence.

"How'd you get a name like the Martian Princess?" said Dave.

The Princess made a noise that was a combination of a laugh and a sigh. "Do you know anything about the Children of Mars?" she said.

"Some."

"OK, good, then you know that people with red hair are descendents of the ancient race that once lived on Mars, right?"

"Uh, right."

"And the more red the hair is, the stronger the birthright. So partly it's because my hair is very red and very long. I look more Martian than most."

"I must say that you look like a Princess," said Dave.

"Hmmm. Yes, that's what people tell me. Anyway, it's mostly because of my Dad."

"Who's your Dad?"

"He's that guy over there," she said, pointing at the balding man. "He's called the Emperor of Mars. He organized the Children of Mars, and is the leader of the group. I don't know how he managed to get that title for himself, but since he did, I became a Princess."

Dave chuckled. Bert came up to the table, munching a Tringo, and growled at Dave. "You lost, Peter won. Next round," he said.

Dave looked helplessly at the Princess. "Don't let me keep you from your game," she said, standing up.

Dave reluctantly wandered back to the table where Peter, Paul, and Bert waited to begin the next round of Icehouse. The Martian Princess followed, and watched as they played. She stood beside Dave, and during the game they quietly continued their conversation.

Jim, who had been enviously regarding Dave's successful interaction with the Martian Princess, finally decided to leave. He paid Mandy for his drink, tucked his City Paper under his arm, and wandered out into the empty streets.

Around 11 o'clock, the Emperor of Mars and his fellow gamers stood up and made ready to leave. Before joining them, the Martian Princess dug into the small canvas shoulder bag she carried and extracted a business card. It was red, and had imprinted on it a picture of Mars. Above this was "The Martian Princess" and at the bottom was an address and a telephone number. She handed the card to Dave, smiled broadly, and then quickly joined the others as they slipped out of the Saturn Cafe.

Chapter 48

Bill was like a moth, drawn incessantly to a flickering fluorescent lamp.

Yet he was also like a child, forced to stay at the dinner table until he'd finished his vegetables but unable to bring himself to eat them.

He was completely obsessed with the Time Shifter. He wanted desperately to push the button, but was too afraid of the consequences to do it very often.

Almost every evening, and for large parts of many days, he would sit, for hours, with his finger poised over the big green "ENGAGE" button, attempting to summon the nerve to push the button, just to see what would happen.

Sometimes he did, and strange things occurred.

On other nights, he could not bring himself to do it.

Either way, he always went to bed with a stiff arm.

The Time Shifter had done some odd things. A friend of his who had suffered a broken arm had instead suffered a broken leg. An automobile collision in the street two blocks down had become an incident in which an ambulance had run over and killed a dog. A grease fire at "Dollars to Donuts" had changed into a food poisoning episode in which three people had gone to the hospital to get their stomachs pumped. One morning Bill found Suzanne rehearsing for a part in "Jesus Christ Superstar" that she'd previously been turned down for.

Sometimes when Bill pushed the button it took several days for him to unravel what had happened. And sometimes, he never found out at all.

And he began to hate the machine. He hated the grip it had on him. It tormented him. Even when he wasn't sitting before it, attempting to get up the nerve to use it, a vision of it thrashed around in his brain. And he felt oppressive guilt about the negative changes that had occurred.

He'd been like this for weeks.

Then one evening, it all came to an end.

He'd been sitting there, staring at the Time Shifter, for 2 hours and 35 minutes. Then, he took a deep breath, clenched his teeth, clamped his eyes shut, and pushed the button.

Flash!

The usual charred smell was stronger this time. Bill slowly opened his eyes. And to his astonishment, he saw that the Time Shifter itself had changed!

Whereas before it had had six clocks, now it only had five. Much of the wiring looked different. The control box had a couple of new indicators, and several of the old indicators seemed to have changed.

Bill sat down, very very slowly, and looked at the new Time Shifter.

The Time Shifter had shifted. Bill knew that the only way to find out what it did now was to push the button and see.

But his apprehension about doing so was now far greater than it had ever been before.

Bill sat up for hours and hours, drinking coffee, looking at the machine, and thinking.

Finally, at 6 minutes after 4 o'clock in the morning, he pressed the button. This time the flash was fainter, and there was no burning smell at all.

And Bill flew forward into the Future.

Chapter 49

On Saturday, Dave called the Princess. They made small talk for several minutes, and then Dave asked if she was free for dinner.

"Sure," she said. "But I should let you know right away that I'm a vegetarian."

"Oh, uh, OK," said Dave. "Is that because Martians don't eat meat?"

"No, it has nothing to do with that," she said. "I just don't believe in eating animals."

"Well, that's cool," said Dave. "I like meat myself, but I'm sure we can cope. Let's see... how's about pizza?"

"Sure, that's fine, I love pizza."

"Great. I'll pick you up at eight, OK?"

"Yes."

Within 30 seconds of hanging up the phone, Dave was out the door, and at 8:29, he and the Princess ate pizza. He had pepperoni and she had mushroom and olive.

Afterwards, they talked.

She told him things about Mars, and her father, and his ideas about ancient Martian race memories stored in the subconscious of people with red hair.

"Sometimes I think it's all a bunch of ridiculous nonsense," she confided, "but at other times I think there might be something to it.

When a bunch of different artists and sculptors, people who have nothing in common except for the color of their hair, when they create works of art that seem somehow similar and related, doesn't it seem... well, it sort of makes you wonder, doesn't it?"

"I suppose."

"Take a look at this," said the Princess. She dug into the small canvas shoulder bag which she carried and pulled out a small rock-like thing.

The object was made out of stainless steel, but was stained with black marks and fused lumps of metal and had a very rough and unpolished appearance. Its shape was that of a flattened sphere, two inches in diameter; two saucers of metal joined together like a clamshell. It resembled a rock more than anything else, though it could also be compared to a charcoal briquette. One might see it lying in the grass of a forest, or in the sand on a beach, or in the mud at a skyscraper construction site, and give it not another thought.

The Princess handed the object to Dave. He looked at it, and scrunched up his face the way a child does when presented with a bowl of cauliflower. "What is it?" he said. His voice was filled with disgust.

"Shake it," commanded the Princess.

Dave skeptically obeyed. He shook the rock gently, and was amazed. This hunk of ugly fused metal produced beautiful sounds. It made a gentle, tingling sound, like wind chimes in the distance. The sounds were magical and ethereal, faint but quite undeniable. And it took Dave away, to another time and another place, and he thought of his childhood, and of the sweet smell of flowers, and of twinkling stars in the deep blue sky.

A broad smile spread across Dave's face. "Wow," he said, laughing. "That's really cool."

He had shaken it very gently, and it had produced just a few tiny notes. The Princess encouraged him to shake it vigorously, and they heard a symphony of magical sound.

"What is it?" Dave asked.

"It's called 'Stardust,' " said the Princess. "It's a sound sculpture by a man named Reinhold Marxhausen."

Dave shook the Stardust repeatedly, marveling at the beautiful sounds it produced.

"Here," said the Princess, "Strike it with this fork." Dave did so, and the metal stone became a bell. "Now hold it to your ear," she said. The stone continued to resonate, gong-like, for a long time in Dave's ear.

"That's amazing," said Dave.

"Now this," said the Princess, "just doesn't seem to me to be something of this Earth, at least not of this civilization. It's things like this that make me believe Dad's crackpot theories. I can almost believe that this is really a recreated piece of a different civilization, that this really belongs millions of miles away, on Mars."

Dave didn't reply. He was still marveling at the Stardust, shaking it and holding it to his ear.

The Princess let Dave play with the Stardust as they rode home on the subway, but when they got back to her place, she demanded its return, and stowed it away again in her canvas bag.

They went inside her apartment. "Would you like some tea?" said the Princess.

"What kind?" said Dave.

"Hmmmmmm," said the Princess. It was a soft, purring, laughing noise. "I have many kinds of tea. Come into the kitchen and pick one."

The Princess had 29 different varieties of tea. They ranged across her refrigerator and also occupied some of the cabinets. Dave was daunted, but finally selected something called "Emperor's Choice."

"Ha!" said the Princess, "That's a good tea. It's my Dad's favorite."

"Naturally," said Dave.

Dave sat drinking tea and chatting with the Princess for much of the night.

Around one o'clock, she decided it was time for him to go. He protested, but went to the door anyway. "Thanks for dinner," she said, gently maneuvering him outside. "Call me tomorrow." She gave him a quick kiss, and then scurried back inside her apartment and closed the door behind her.

Chapter 50

At 11:33 PM, a telephone rang in an apartment on the tenth floor of a high rise on the east side of town, about two blocks north of the Destiny Boulevard subway station. Even though four people were sitting in the apartment, listening to the phone as it rang, not one of them moved to answer it.

After the fourth ring, an answering machine cut in.

"Hi there. Either we ain't home or we're playing Icehouse and therefore will not answer the phone. So leave a message."

After the machine beeped, the Four heard Jim talking to the machine.

"Hey dudes, have any of you seen Bill? He's been acting really strange for the last few weeks, and today he didn't come to work, and his latest contraption is gone, and no one's seen him, so we're starting to get worried. Please give us a call."

Peter played a couple of his pyramids and said, "Maybe he's traveling through time."

Paul nodded and made of grunt of agreement.

Chapter 51

The Emperor of Mars lived in a very large apartment building in the heart of the City. The lobby of the building interfaced directly with the Digital Plateau subway station, located at the transfer point between the green line and the brown line, in the southeast corner of the downtown sector.

Dave and the Princess rode the escalator up to the lobby from the deep confines of the subway. The Princess stood on the step above Dave, facing him, and looking down the stairs as they moved up them.

"What have I told you so far about my father?" she asked.

Dave thought for a moment, and said "Not much. He's the Emperor of Mars, and you're the Princess. I guess you've said that the whole "Children of Mars" thing was his idea, too."

"Correct. Anything else?"

"Let's see. You've said his favorite tea is 'Emperor's Choice,' and I also know that he doesn't like noise when he plays Icehouse."

"Quite true. Anything else?"

"No, that's about it," said Dave, a bit vacantly. He'd become distracted, because they were approaching the top of the escalator, and the Princess didn't seem to be paying any attention. Would she stumble when the moving stairs met the stationary floor? Would her floor length skirt get caught in the machinery? Should he say something about the situation? If he did, but she was well aware of it, she might get mad at him for fussing too much. If he didn't, and she fell over, would she blame him for not warning her? Finally he decided to keep his mouth shut. She's probably ridden this escalator thousands of times, he reasoned, and she knows exactly how long the trip is. She can probably disembark safely even with her eyes closed.

"There's something else I should tell you," said the Princess, turning around and stepping off the escalator just as it came to the top.

"What?"

"My father invented Icehouse."

Bombs exploded inside of Dave's skull. He stopped dead and stared at the Princess. After a lapse of silent seconds, he said "Wow. That's amazing."

The Princess shrugged her shoulders. "Nah, not really," she said.

They strolled through the lobby of the building, breezed past the desk, pointedly ignoring the sign that read "All visitors must sign in," and made their way over to the bank of elevators.

An elevator was open and waiting, and Dave started towards it. "No," said the Princess, pointing, "We have to get *that* one."

Dave asked why, but she didn't answer him.

Finally, the correct elevator came, and they got in. The Princess produced her keys and confronted the button panel. At the top of the rows of buttons was an unlabeled keyhole. She inserted a key into this hole, and the elevator doors slid closed. The little room lurched upwards.

When the doors finally opened again, they led into a well appointed living room. Dave, who had expected to see a hallway, was again taken by surprise.

"Your Dad has the whole floor? And a private elevator?"

The Princess gave out a sort of trilling laugh and sang, "Yes."

The elevator entrance was on a small landing in the corner of the living room. The Princess moved softly down the two steps and into the room. "Hello, Daddy!" she called out.

Someone yelled something from a distant room, but it was garbled and incomprehensible.

The Princess padded off toward the kitchen, but Dave walked around the room, looking with amazement at the decor.

The walls were covered with pictures of Mars. There were big blow-up photos, taken by spacecraft, and full color paintings of the classical Mars, its surface etched with canals. There were also numerous pictures of Martians and things of a Martian nature: various different visions of the tripod fighting machines of H.G. Wells, different interpretations of the cities of Mars described by Ray Bradbury, and numerous cartoons, drawings, and paintings of Little Green Men from countless different sources.

On one side of the room, some models sat on a kind of display table. A huge globe of Mars dominated the display, though similarly prominent were several recreations of the flying, stingray-shaped fighting machines from George Pal's film version of "The War of the Worlds."

The Princess called out from the kitchen, "You want something to eat?"

Dave snapped out of his daze. "Um, sure!" he called out, as he followed the sound of her voice to the kitchen.

It was a big kitchen, and it was loaded with food. If you could call it food. Nutrition didn't seem to be the Emperor's biggest concern. By the look of the cupboards, the fridge, and the trash, he seemed to eat mostly junk. The inventory included bags of chips, boxes of pastries, bottles of soda, and cartons of candy. The trash can overflowed with empty pizza and doughnut boxes, and the fridge was well stocked with leftover Chinese food in those little cardboard cartons. The freezer was full of frozen pizzas, TV dinners, and "Boil-in-a-Bag" style frozen foods. A couple of frozen "Ready-to-Thaw" desserts had also been shoe-horned into the freezer, and when Dave first came in he'd found the Princess setting a chocolate cream pie out on the counter to thaw.

"Disgusting, isn't it?" said the Princess.

"Guess his mom never made him eat his vegetables," said Dave.

"Take whatever looks good to you," said the Princess. "He makes a point of keeping plenty on hand for guests."

Dave nodded gravely and carefully surveyed the environment. He contemplated eating a couple of Ho-Hos but eventually took nothing except a Coke. The Princess put some water on to boil, and then, seeing that Dave was ready to move on, led him out of the kitchen and down the hall.

They passed several large, darkened rooms, working their way toward the back of the flat. Dave noticed that the view through the windows was vast and impressive, and figured that they must be on the top floor.

At last they located a well lit room, blazing like a lighthouse in the otherwise dark apartment. The Princess rapped on the doorframe and went in. "Hello, Daddy!" she chirped, and kissed her father on the forehead.

The Emperor of Mars was sitting before a computer terminal, typing away at something. The room he was working in appeared to be a study, the walls lined with bookshelves, each crammed with books. The Emperor himself was wearing a long robe, made of reddish brown cloth and marked here and there with thick black lines. After studying it a moment, Dave realized that it was meant to be reminiscent of the Classical Mars: a red body with canals described upon it.

Dave and the Princess stood in the doorway, waiting, while the Emperor basically ignored them, typing away at his computer. After

ANDREW LOONEY

about a minute, he seemed to reach an acceptable stopping place, and leaned back.

"Hi, kid," he said, "Who's this?"

"This is Dave," said the Princess, with a slight bow.

"OK," said the Emperor. He extended his hand to Dave, who took it and shook it. "Pleased to meet you."

Dave blurted out, "Is it true that you invented Icehouse?"

"Of course it's true!" said the Emperor. "Well, partly anyway. It was my idea, but a friend of mine had a hand in working out the rules."

"Who?"

"A guy we call Dr Cool," said the Emperor, enigmatically.

"Does he live here, too?"

"Oh, no, of course not. Actually, right now he's living in New York, though he rides his motorcycle down this way fairly often."

Dave's head was spinning. "This is amazing! I guess you guys are about the best players around!"

The Emperor gave a noncommittal grunt. Then he said, "We're OK. But just because we invented the game doesn't mean we're *good* at it."

"Well, I'd, just, um," Dave stumbled over his words. "I'd love to play against you guys sometime, even though, you know, I'm sure I'd lose."

"We can probably work in a game at some point."

"Wow! That'd be great!"

"Uh-huh. Did you see the Collection?"

"You mean the art out in the living room?"

"No, I mean the sets." He turned to the Princess. "Did you show him the sets?"

She shook her head, no.

"OK, then show him the sets! Then I hope you'll excuse me, I have a lot to do. Nice meeting you, Dave. I'll see about getting you into a game at some point."

With that, the Emperor turned back to his computer.

The Princess led Dave out of the study and into another room. This room was in the corner of the apartment and had huge picture windows on two walls. Dave had a dazzling view of the lights of the city below. Then the Princess turned on the lights and showed him the Collection.

Icehouse sets! On the non-window walls were shelves and shelves and shelves, each shelf covered with Icehouse sets, lined up for display. The Emperor had collected sets of every type, every material imaginable. Plastic pyramids in a huge rainbow of colors, wood sets of painted and stained colors as well as numerous exotic woods, machined metals of different hues, some anodized in bright shades, pottery and hand made clay pieces, and pyramids made of stone! Dave was particularly enchanted by a set made of polished malachite. There were

72

sets with odd patterns painted upon them, plastic sets with strange things embedded in them, and even a set of candles in the shape of Icehouse pieces. Dave was truly amazed. The Princess heard her tea kettle whistling and silently disappeared. Eventually, overwhelmed and in a bit of a daze, Dave followed the Princess back to the kitchen.

She sat at the kitchen table, drinking tea. "Would you like Tea?" she asked.

"Um, no, I'm still drinking my Coke."

"The pie is still a little frozen in the middle, but we can go ahead and eat some if you'd like."

"Yeah, OK."

The Princess cut them a couple of slices of pie.

"Yeah, it's still kind of frozen in the middle," said Dave.

The Princess nodded.

A large black cat wandered in and ate a bit from a bowl on the floor in the corner.

Dave said, "Does anyone live here besides him?"

"No. Just him and the cats."

"But this place is huge!" said Dave.

"Well, he has a lot of stuff," said the Princess. "Besides, he sometimes has several house guests at a time, and he likes to have room for them."

After they finished their pie, the Princess indicated that they should go.

Dave asked if they should say goodbye to the Emperor, but she said, no, they didn't need to, they'd already been dismissed. So when the elevator came, they left without saying another word.

Chapter 52

At one minute after two in the morning, Maria crouched behind a bush in the backyard of the Asylum. Behind the bush was a small metal structure that protruded from the ground a few feet away from the house. This was an air vent for Torrence's bomb shelter. The air vent could be closed, or it could be opened to allow air to flow in normally. It had originally been designed to use filters, which were supposed to keep radioactive dust out of the shelter in times of crisis, but Torrence had never been able to find replacements. Despite the lack of these filters, Torrence always left the vent open. With it closed, the shelter was stuffy and the air quickly became stale.

"Torrence!" whispered Maria into the vent.

The vent also conducted sound wonderfully, and allowed visitors to talk to whomever was in the shelter without disturbing the other inmates of the Asylum. It was a perfect intercom.

"Torrence!" whispered Maria, a bit more loudly.

Torrence had been sleeping. "Hello?" he said, a bit groggily, "Is that you, Maria?"

"Yes!" whispered Maria. "Let's go get some Ice Cream!"

Torrence groaned. But it was not a negative groan. It was the groan of a father who pretends to protest when his children are begging for one more bedtime story or yet another piggy back ride. It was a grin masquerading as a groan.

"Oh, come on!" pleaded Maria, reading Torrence's mood and playing along with it. "Please?"

"Very well," said Torrence.

"Yay!" said Maria, forgetting to be quiet.

Torrence gathered himself together, and eventually emerged, quietly shutting the front door behind him. While waiting for him, Maria had strolled around the house, enjoying the night. It was a cool November night, and the air smelled clean and crisp.

Torrence and Maria strolled along the sidewalk toward the Geddes Point subway station. Maria was full of energy, having just gotten away from work, and went skipping ahead, and running back, and bouncing around Torrence in circles. Torrence strode quickly, purposefully forward, talking big steps, with his hands in his pockets and his mouth in a grin.

They got on the subway and rode north, to the Industry Circle station. After a five minute walk, they slid into a booth at the Henderson Diner and glanced briefly at the menus. Maria ordered a banana split, and Torrence ordered a black and white, a vanilla milkshake served in a goblet lined with hot fudge.

Maria talked up a storm, telling Torrence about her day at work and about whatever else came into her mind. Torrence listened, telling her things when he was able to get a word in, and answering questions that she had occasion to ask. Then the ice cream came, and they stopped talking in order to eat.

Torrence stirred up his black and white, and slurpingly drank a few mouthfuls. Then he smiled to himself as he thought about where he was and what he was doing. He'd been dragged out of bed in the middle of a chilly November night in order to eat, of all things, ice cream. It was ridiculous! But he couldn't have been happier about it.

Maria loaded up a spoon with ice cream, whipped cream, and a big hunk of banana. As she chewed it, she looked across at Torrence and wondered what he was thinking. Was he just humoring her whimsical nature by going out to get ice cream with her, or was he actually enjoying the outing as much as she was? And did it matter?

Torrence thought about the events of the previous two months. He'd been spending practically all of his free time with Maria, and was thoroughly enjoying it. And he suddenly realized that, during this time, he'd almost never seen the Four. More surprisingly, he found himself realizing that he didn't even care about them anymore. His attitude had changed completely. He no longer had any interest in hanging around with them, or in being accepted by them. They didn't matter to him at all anymore. And while he took a certain amount of smug pleasure in this realization, he also found it rather strange.

Maria also found her mind wandering back, thinking about the time before she and Torrence began dating. She remembered her futile attempts to attract Dave's attention, and smiled to herself. She wondered if he'd ever been aware of her interest in him. She wondered if anything could ever have happened between her and Dave, and if it would have been as good as what she had going now with Torrence. Then reminded herself that it didn't matter, and smiled happily at the man across the table from her.

Torrence took another drink of his black and white and got a dollop of hot fudge on his nose. Maria laughed at him, and then wiped the fudge off with her napkin.

After they'd finished eating, they sat holding hands across the table for a long time. Finally, they went back to the Asylum, where, eventually, they went to sleep.

Chapter 53

Dave woke. He woke slowly, coming out of a dream, finding himself unclear as to what had been the dream and what was reality. At first he didn't know where he was. The bed and the room were unfamiliar. Curled up next to him, he suddenly realized, was the Martian Princess. Then he remembered. He was sleeping at her apartment. He'd taken her to dinner and a movie, then they'd gone back to her place for tea, and they'd sat around talking, and it became late, and... they'd made love for the first time. It had been wonderful.

The room seemed very dark. Dave squinted at a digital clock on the dresser, and saw that it was 4:30 AM. He rolled away from the clock and shut his eyes.

Dave suddenly felt aware of something. He opened his eyes and held them open for several seconds, then clamped them shut again.

There was someone in the room.

Dave thought about this for a bit. Who could be in the room? Was he dreaming? Was his imagination having a bit of fun at his expense? Slowly he opened his eyes again, slowly and only enough to see into the corner.

A woman was standing in the corner, facing the window, looking out into the night. It was very dark in the corner, but Dave could see her nonetheless, very faintly, as if she were illuminated by glow-in-the-dark paint. She seemed to be wearing a long dress with a full skirt.

Dave shut his eyes again and tried to think. He couldn't believe what he was seeing—it was ridiculous. Yet he was certain he was awake. He opened his eyes again.

The woman was standing with her arms folded, gazing out of the window. As Dave watched, she shifted her stance, dropping her right arm to her side and putting her left hand onto the window frame to lean against. Dave noted that she was rather tall, but then realized that she was actually short and was floating in the air, about two feet off the floor. He clamped his eyes shut again, and shivered. He pulled the covers more tightly around him, and then ever so slowly, he opened his eyes once more.

The woman was gone. Faint moonlight shone in through the window, but the corner where he'd seen the woman was completely enshrouded in darkness.

Chapter 54

The digital alarm clock blared. The Princess clambered over Dave, reaching up onto the dresser to shut it off. "Good morning!" she said to him. "Sleep OK?"

Dave felt groggy, but delighted to find himself waking up in the same bed as the Princess. A smile slashed across his face. "Mmm, yes," he said. He slid his arms around her and they kissed.

As they dressed, images of the woman in the corner blasted into Dave's brain. He said "Something strange happened last night."

The Princess laughed. "Oh?" she asked.

"Yes. I think I saw something strange."

"Oh!" The Princess changed her tone, from sarcasm to surprise. "Did you see Alyson?"

"Um," Dave stumbled, "I don't know. Maybe."

"Was she looking out of the window, or sitting in a chair reading?"

"Looking out of the window." said Dave.

"That's Alyson," said the Princess. "She's our ghost."

"Really," said Dave. "Then I wasn't dreaming."

"Oh, no, not at all. I've seen her many times. She's definitely real."

"But," Dave stammered, "I don't believe in ghosts."

The Princess laughed, her voice trilling musically. "Well, you'd better start!" she proclaimed.

Chapter 55

Peter, Paul, and Bert sat at their usual table in the Saturn Cafe, playing Icehouse. Icehouse with three players is definitely not as good as with four, and as a result, they played rather apathetically. Dave had told them earlier that he wouldn't be hanging out with them this evening, since he had a date with someone he called 'The Princess'. So The Four were only three.

Peter leaned back in his chair, and just as he did so, he heard an odd popping sort of sound. To his amazement, he saw Bill suddenly materialize in the Saturn Cafe, standing a couple of yards away from the Pit. He ran over to the table where the Three sat, halfheartedly playing Icehouse.

"Norman!" he shouted, "Look!"

Peter was instantly out of his chair, cavorting around Bill. "Bill!" he shouted, "What happened to you? Where have you been?"

Various other Cafe patrons looked on this scene with distaste. Paul stood up, and tugged on Peter's arm. "Hey, man, keep it down. You're being uncool."

Peter sat down and attempted to restrain himself. Bill sat down, too.

"I've been in the Future," said Bill.

"Yeah, your Time Machine worked, right?"

"Yes," said Bill, "and look!" He held out a piece of metal.

It was the about the size of a normal piece of paper, although slightly longer. It seemed to be a solid plate of white metal, about an eighth of an inch thick. Words and a picture were etched into the metal. It seemed like a very permanent printed document.

"This is a patent," said Bill, "U.S. Patent Number 6,474,650 to be exact." On closer examination of the plate, Peter noticed the number along with the title "Mechanism for Traveling Through Time." The patent bore Bill's name and featured a drawing of a device not unlike the one he had shown them in the Asylum a couple of months before.

Bill took the metal plate back from Peter, and held it, gently, in his hands. "My first patent," he said. His voice was reverent, awed. "I've been waiting for this for many, many years. I'm a real inventor now."

"Well, congratulations!" said Peter. Bert and Paul echoed the sentiment.

"Thank you, thank you," said Bill.

"What's the deal with the metal paper?" said Paul.

"Hmm? Oh! This is how documents are stored now. I mean, in the Future." He handed the plate to Paul. Paul noticed a series of small numbered squares imprinted in a row along the bottom of the plate. "You see," said Bill, "the words and pictures are not actually etched onto the metal, it just looks like they are." He took the metal plate back from Paul and touched a couple of the numbered squares. The etchings on the metal plate vanished and were instantly replaced by a completely different set of words and pictures. "This document can store 4096 pages of printed text, and display any of them instantly. It can also be reprogrammed with different pages. It looks just as good as regular printed paper, but it takes up less space, is completely reusable, and doesn't require the destruction of trees."

"Wow!" said Paul.

Bill leaned towards them, sort of conspiratorially. "It's put photocopying completely out of business. Man, I sure wish I had the patent on *this*!"

The others laughed, and Bill stood up.

"Where are you going?" asked Peter.

"To see my parents," said Bill. "Got to tell them the news!"

"But when will you be coming home?"

"Home?" asked Bill, somewhat confused. Then he said "Oh," and sat down again. "Norman, I live in the Future now." He paused, letting this sink in.

"You mean you're never coming back?" asked Peter.

"Not permanently. I'll be back from time to time, you know, to visit, and to do research... but I doubt if I'll ever actually live in this time period again."

Peter looked glum. Bert ate a Tringo.

"Well," said Bill, standing up again, "I really do have to go. Sorry to rush off so quickly, but I'm a very busy man these days." He pulled a small device out of his pocket, a device about the size of a pocket calculator, only thicker. He pressed some of its buttons, and then turned back to face Peter and the others. "See you later," he said, and waved. Then he pressed another button on his little device, and vanished.

Suddenly, Bert said, "Hey, wait a minute! We should get him to take us through time somewhere!"

"Yeah!" the others agreed fervently. But it was too late; Bill was gone.

Chapter 56

Saturday morning. Mindless cartoons became splattered, one by one, onto Television screens in living rooms all over the City.

However, in the apartment of the Android Sisters, Life was slow in resuming. All three slept very late. Eventually, Mandy crawled out of bed and into the shower. Somewhat later, Cindy staggered out to the living room, retrieved the newspaper from the hall, and collapsed with it onto the couch. Lastly, Wendy wandered absently into the kitchen, located a box of cereal, a blue glass bowl, a silver teaspoon, and a carton of milk. From these raw materials, she constructed a breakfast.

Mandy emerged from her room, showered, dressed and alive. By this time it was almost noon. Mandy took the elevator down to the lobby to collect the mail. When she returned, she tossed the mail with disgust onto the table in the dining room, where Wendy munched cereal.

"Nothing good in the mail," she announced. She sat down at the table across from Wendy.

Silence dominated for awhile, disrupted only by the sounds of Wendy's breakfast and Cindy's newspaper.

"Hey," said Wendy, as she refilled her bowl, "I had a really weird dream last night. We were in a car, and we were driving across the desert. It was a nice car, a white convertible, and we had the top down and we were going like a hundred miles an hour, and the wind was whipping through our hair. And we had the Atomic Bomb with us, you know, the one the Four gave us, and we were taking it somewhere. I don't really remember now why or who, but I think somebody needed it for something, so we were rushing across the desert to deliver it to him. So there we were, driving the Atomic Bomb across the desert." She paused, pouring more milk onto her cereal.

"The next thing I remember was that we came to the Border and were stopped at a customs checkpoint. They looked over our passports and papers and junk, but luckily they didn't search the car, and we had the Bomb covered up, so they let us through. Then, all of a sudden we were stopped by some train robbers. This big old train just blasted across the road in front of us, and we stopped and they stopped and these bank robbers, like from an old TV western, you know, with handkerchiefs on their faces and a gun in each hand, these bank robbers jumped off the train and pointed their guns at us and told us to hand over the Atomic Bomb! So we gave them the Bomb and they jumped back onto the train and chugged off. It was an old train, you know, the steam locomotive kind, but there weren't any train tracks, it was just driving normally, like a car or something. Anyway, we started to drive away, but we couldn't, because our car was up on cinder blocks. They'd stolen our wheels, too! So we had to hitchhike. We got a ride to a truck stop in a big eighteen wheeler, but the food at the truck stop was really expensive, like 35 dollars for a cup of coffee, and the breakfast special was $175, so we couldn't afford to eat anything, and we were really hungry. I think something else happened with some of the truck stop waitresses, but I don't really remember. It was strange."

Silence reigned over the room once more. Neither Cindy nor Mandy could think of any response to Wendy's dream. But then, Mandy turned around and looked up at the Atomic Bomb, which was perched, out of the way and all but forgotten, on a high shelf. "Hmm," she said. "That makes me wonder. Do you think we could sell that thing? Maybe someone would like to buy it, maybe we could get a few bucks for it. We can always use extra cash."

Cindy put down her newspaper. "Who'd want it?" she said, somewhat incredulous.

"I don't know," said Mandy. "In some ways it's kind of neat. I'll bet there's somebody out there who'd like to have it."

"But it's useless!" insisted Cindy.

"Oh, I don't know," said Wendy. "The timer on it is pretty good."

When they'd first gotten the bomb, Wendy had tried to find some way of putting it to good use. About the only thing she'd been able to think of was to use it as a kitchen timer. This was great when you needed to cook something for one minute, but was a bit of a pain for marking longer periods of time, since the bomb only counted 60 seconds. Cooking something for a longer time required constantly resetting the bomb and re-pushing the detonation button. Wendy had quickly gotten tired of this, and scrounged up a regular kitchen timer to use instead.

Mandy said, "Maybe someone would want it for a film project or something. After all, it does look like a real Atomic Bomb."

"Well, I'd be happy to be rid of it," said Cindy. "It gives me the creeps."

Mandy located a pad and a pen. She read her words aloud as she wrote them: "For Sale, one Atomic Bomb. $100.00 or best offer. Call 301-441-1019." She scrounged up an envelope and a stamp, dug up the previous week's City Paper, wrote the address of the paper's classifieds desk on the envelope, and sealed it. Then she slipped out into the hall and dropped the envelope into the mailslot. Whoosh! It fell into a box at the bottom of the slot, many floors down.

"We'll just see what happens," she said upon returning. Cindy was still reading her paper, and Wendy was washing up her breakfast dishes. Neither said anything else about the Atomic Bomb.

Chapter 57

Jim made himself a chicken salad sandwich and locked himself up inside his closet. He had just gotten the new City Paper, and as he bit into his sandwich he turned directly to the "Personals" section.

He scanned the column of fine print ads, dropping sandwich crumbs on the paper as he went. "SWM... SWM... DWM... SWM... SWF loves shopping, sports... SWM... SBM... SWF, attractive, independent, loves soap operas... SJM... DWM... SWM... GWM... BiWF ISO similar BiWF... Rubenesque SWF... MWF seeks MWM for discreet encounters... SBF... SWM... Religious SWF... SWM..."

He was about to give up on this week's offerings when he found an ad that read:

Tremendous SWF, 30, independent, intelligent, and creative, seeks similar SWM with whom to listen to music, go out to dinner, see movies, and ride rollercoasters. Non-smokers and cat-lovers preferred. Must have good sense of humor. Write to me NOW! Box 761.

Jim wondered if the word "Tremendous" were a euphemism for "Fat," but in spite of his slight misgiving, he decided to send her something. He pulled out a sheet of stationery and started to write a letter: "Dear SWF, I saw your ad, and you sound like a fun person so I decided to write to you." Jim read this sentence and then crumpled up the sheet of paper. "It sounds stupid," he said aloud to himself. "Every letter she gets probably sounds like that."

He sat for a long time twirling his pencil around in his hand, trying to think of some way of writing an introductory letter that didn't sound boring and stupid.

Finally he decided not to send a letter at all. He concluded that he needed something that would grab her attention, that would make his letter stand out from the other ten she'd probably receive. He decided to send an envelope containing only an assortment of odd things. He had a cigar box containing small clippings, cards, and slips of paper, which he acquired and saved from all over the place. He'd often toss one of these items in with letters he sent to friends and relatives. This letter, he decided, would contain nothing except an assortment of artifacts such as these.

He dug around in his cigar box, pulling out choice items. A "Colonel Mustard" card from an old "Clue" game. An "Inspected by #12" slip. A picture he'd cut out of a newspaper, depicting a mushroom cloud rising above the Nevada desert during a bomb test in the 1950s. A carnival ticket reading "KEEP THIS COUPON * IT IS VALUABLE." A playing card, the eight of hearts. A matchbook cover from "Trader Flip's," a Polynesian restaurant. A photograph of him, taken the previous Christmas, wearing a Santa Claus hat. A yellow slip of paper with some mathematical formulas written on it, which he had found on the floor of "Dollars to Donuts" a few days before. A Cracker Jack prize, a tiny booklet of brain teasers. A full color photo of the unblinking statues on Easter Island, clipped out of a magazine. And lastly, a Bazooka Joe comic.

Jim placed all of these items into a business size envelope. He wrote his name and return address in the corner, but it then took him a while to figure out how to address the envelope correctly so that it would properly get to the person who'd placed the ad. This done, he put a stamp on the envelope and strolled with it out into the nighttime.

As he tossed it into the corner mailbox, he thought "That ought to make her sit up and take notice."

Chapter 58

At a dozen minutes after midnight, the Princess's princess telephone rang. She and Dave were in an intimate embrace, but it was after the event not before, and so the interruption was not poorly timed.

She answered on the third ring. "Yes?"

She was sitting up in bed, with her beautiful red hair cascading down her back.

"I suppose so," she said into the receiver, sounding rather annoyed.

Dave, curled up nearby, reached out and stroked her long hair, then rubbed his hand along her smooth soft shoulders.

"You mean now?" This time she sounded rather downtrodden, as if resigned to her fate. She squirmed away from Dave's caresses.

"Yes. OK. No. No, that's OK. All right. Bye."

She sighed deeply. Then she hung up the phone and got out of bed. "Get dressed," she said.

Dave didn't move. "Why?" he asked.

"That was Dad. We're supposed to meet him in 45 minutes, downtown at the Henderson Diner."

Dave groaned. "Why does it have to be now? Can't it wait until tomorrow?"

"That's not how things work with Dad," said the Princess.

Dave saw that he couldn't protest. They got dressed and caught a subway train.

When they arrived, just after 1 AM, they saw that the Emperor was already there. He was drinking a chocolate milk shake.

They went in and sat down.

The Emperor said, "Thanks for coming. You guys want anything?"

The Princess said "Toast."

Dave shrugged. "I don't know. Are there menus?"

The Emperor yelled, "Marty? One toast and one menu!"

Someone in the back yelled an unclear but positive sounding response.

"So, daddy," said the Princess, "What's so urgent?"

The Emperor looked at Dave. "You wanted to challenge me and the Doctor, right?"

Dave was startled. He felt as if he'd just been accused of a crime. "Um, yes," he admitted, rather sheepishly.

"OK, then. The Doctor will be here shortly. Did you bring your set?"

Dave frowned. "No."

The Emperor shrugged. "That's OK, I've got a spare."

Marty came out with the toast and the menu, dropped them on the table, and shuffled away.

As the Princess munched her toast and the Emperor drank his shake, Dave looked through the menu. He said "Um, cheese omelet?"

The Emperor yelled, "Marty? Cheese omelet!"

Marty yelled an unclear but positive sounding response from somewhere in the back.

The Emperor poured the last of his shake out of the cannister and into the goblet. He lifted the goblet halfway to his mouth and then stopped. Holding it in midair, he fixed his gaze on Dave. "Dave," he said, "Do you draw?"

Dave thought for a moment, and said, "No, not really."

"Paint?"

"No."

"Write poems?"

"Nope."

"Compose music?"

"Uh-uh."

"Take photographs?"

Dave had finally had enough of this interrogation. "Why are you asking all of these questions?"

The Emperor flashed a peevish glance at his daughter. "Hasn't she told you?"

The Princess was tracing the boomerang shapes of the Formica countertop pattern with her index finger and did not look up.

The Emperor sighed heavily. He took a long swig of milk shake, and then set the goblet down on the table with a loud thunk. "You know about my theory of Mars, don't you?"

"Sort of," offered Dave, timidly.

"OK. The idea is that redheads have ancient race memories of Mars buried in their subconscious. These memories can still be tapped into, by thinking creatively. The artist who paints what he thinks is an imaginary alien city might really be seeing, in his mind's eye, a vision of a real city on ancient Mars. Right?"

"Right," said Dave.

"Now these memories can surface in many ways. The ideas for Icehouse, for example, originally came to me in a dream. Right?"

"Right," said Dave.

"So what I'm doing now, what I've been working on for quite a while in fact, is attempting to bring together the creative works of a large number of Martian descendents, to see their creative works collectively, to see if they really add up to anything. I've seen similarities in the work of different Martian artists before, and I'm hoping, that by bringing a lot of such work together, it will add up to a cohesive big picture, a glimpse, if you will, of the ancient civilization of Mars. Right?"

"Right," said Dave.

At about this time, a motorcycle pulled up in front of the Diner.

"OK. To this end, I am organizing an art show, which is set to open in the first week of March at the Teldman Gallery. And whenever I meet a Martian, I always find out what creative work they do, if any, to see how it might fit into the big puzzle of ancient Mars. See?"

"Mmm, yes, I see," said Dave. "It all sounds very logical and scientific."

What Dave thought, however, was "This guy is a total crackpot!"

The door to the Diner opened, and a tall man dressed entirely in black leather strode in. He wore a black motorcycle helmet, black leather jacket, black chaps, black boots, and black gloves. He strode over to the booth, smiled at the Emperor and his party, and started stripping down. He hung his helmet and jacket on the hat rack beside the booth, put his gloves inside the helmet, and sat down. Then he stood up again and extracted from his jacket a thin wooden case. He looked at Dave.

"You must be Dave," he said. "I understand you want to play us." He grinned at the Emperor and then burst out with an evil sounding laugh.

"Yes," admitted Dave.

"Good," he grinned. Then he called out, "Marty? Coffee!"

Marty yelled something incomprehensible from somewhere in the back.

Doctor Cool opened the thin wooden case. It contained fifteen Icehouse pieces, carved from something very black and very shiny.

"Black onyx," said the Doctor, noticing Dave's reaction.

The Emperor had by this time extracted a similar wooden case, and was setting his pieces out on the table. These were made of plaster of paris, and looked rather awful.

"These," said the Emperor, "are the first ever Icehouse pieces. I made them years ago after a particularly vivid dream. Admittedly, they're pretty nasty, but they remain one of my favorite sets."

Dave nodded.

When he'd finished setting up his pieces, the Emperor dug around in his coat, produced a box of plain, ordinary plastic pieces, and handed it over to Dave.

Marty arrived with the omelet and coffee, and they postponed the game until after they had eaten.

When they finally did play, it was a disaster for Dave. He was a good player, but the Doctor and the Emperor really took him to the cleaners. They used strategies and maneuvers that he'd never before dreamed of. And though his defeat embarrassed him, he was inwardly excited by the lessons he'd learned. Boy, he'd show Bert and the twins a few things at their next game!

The Princess had refrained from playing. At the outset of the first game she had produced a paperback novel and had been reading, but as the games wore on she had leaned against the wall and fallen asleep.

Suddenly, the Emperor looked at his watch, stood up, and said "That's it for me, boys, I gotta run."

The Doctor stood up and stretched. "Yeah, I think I'll hit the road, too."

The Emperor walked briskly up to the counter and called for Marty. When Marty emerged, the Emperor gave him some money. Meanwhile, Doctor Cool had been putting his leathers back on.

The inventors of Icehouse got to the door at about the same time. Dave watched through the window as they chattered briefly about something, then went their separate ways. They punctuated their parting with something similar to a handshake, but also different. They had each used both hands, and instead of clasping hands they had gripped wrists. For a brief moment, four hands gripped four wrists. And then they were gone.

Dave woke up the Princess, and took her home.

Chapter 59

Peter, Paul and Umberto entered their apartment building, Peter reading a copy of the City Paper as they walked. They got onto the elevator, disappointed as always to find it already occupied by Doug. Peter made a point of holding the newspaper in front of him, thus avoiding eye contact with Doug. Paul and Bert had to resort to the traditional elevator stance: arms crossed, head lowered, shoulders slumped against the wall.

Fortunately, Doug said nothing. At last the doors squeaked open. Bert and Paul quickly strolled out, but Peter, realizing he was finished with his paper, closed it, folded it, and suddenly handed it to Doug. Doug was startled. Peter dashed through the doors just as they started to close.

The elevator lurched. Doug stood there looking at the City Paper. Then he opened it, flipping through the pages. He found the comics and read them, but found them rather incomprehensible. He came to the classifieds and glanced through them. One caught his eye: "For Sale, one Atomic Bomb. $100.00 or best offer."

Chapter 60

Jim was locked in his closet, reading his City Paper. He casually read the classifieds. His eyes widened at one: "For Sale, one Atomic Bomb. $100.00 or best offer." Then he realized that the phone number was familiar, and quickly figured out why. "The Android Sisters are trying to sell the Bomb that The Four gave them," he said to himself. He found this amusing, and chuckled. Then he turned to the Personals, and read them carefully.

Chapter 61

Friday afternoon in the offices of the Nuclear Regulatory Commission was always a slow time. Many people had already left for the day, and those still around were either working very lethargically, or else were not working at all.

One man sat at his desk, reading a copy of the City Paper.

He came across an ad in the classified section that made his eyes bulge and his heart race.

"For Sale, one Atomic Bomb. $100.00 or best offer."

He shrieked, and called the ad to the attention of his colleagues. They swung into action, making calls, looking up records. Soon they had the answer.

"It's that stupid fake bomb we tracked down a few months ago. It's nothing to worry about... but we better keep the file open anyway."

The NRC office soon returned to its state of drowsy calm.

"See you on Monday," said a couple of employees, as they wandered out the door.

Chapter 62

Mandy opened the kitchen door of the Saturn Cafe and went in. It was 5:00. Her shift was just starting, whereas Wendy had just worked the day shift and was getting ready to go home.

"Hi, Mandy" said Wendy.

"Hi, Wendy" said Mandy.

"Hey, someone called about the Bomb."

"Oh? Who?"

"Some foreign-sounding guy. He had a real thick accent and I had a hard time understanding what he was saying."

"So?"

"So, he started asking me all these questions, like was it a Uranium bomb or a Plutonium bomb, and all kinds of technical stuff I didn't even understand, and finally I said it didn't really work, and you know what?"

"What?"

"He hung up on me!"

"Wow."

"I think he might have been a terrorist."

"Hmm. Well, I gotta get going."

"Yeah, OK, I'll see you later."

Chapter 63

Doug was thinking hard about the ad.

An Atomic Bomb!

Wow!

With an Atomic Bomb, he could...

He could...

Hmm, what could he do?

He could hold up a bank.

Yes!

That's it! Rob a bank, with a nuclear weapon! Threaten to blow up the City unless they gave him lots of money! It would work!

He left the elevator and went to a pay phone. He called the Android Sisters and told them he wanted to buy their bomb. He scrounged up all of the money he had, which was a little over two hundred dollars. He left the building, heading for the subway.

Later that night, he returned home with the Atomic Bomb wrapped up in a sheet. He started to make plans.

Chapter 64

Nineteen days after Jim mailed a random assortment of stuff to a mailstop at the City Paper, he received a letter.

The envelope was a rubber stamp masterpiece. Whoever had sent this to Jim was clearly a collector and fancier of rubber stamps. His address was written into a box drawn in the center of the envelope, and little pictures crammed and crowded themselves into all of the envelope space external to this address box. The rubber stamps depicted many things: faces, dinosaurs, people, trees, stars, planets, cats, birds, cars, flowers, and insects.

Jim opened the letter. Inside was a single sheet of paper, which was also a rubber stamp special. Jim noticed a sea monster, a bulldozer pushing the Earth into a landfill, a Zeppelin, a television set being smashed with a sledgehammer, and a picture of three abstract coffee mugs sliding along a counter, under which were the words "Coffee Races!"

These images surrounded a box into which this was written:

Hi Santa!
I really enjoyed the grab bag. Although you didn't say anything concrete about yourself in your "letter," I think I learned more from it than I did from any of the other 18 letters I got in response to my ad. You seem cool. I'd like to get together. My phone number is 555-4936. Call me NOW!"

The letter was signed not by hand but with a big rubber stamp that said "RHONDA."

The salutation puzzled Jim until he remembered, after a long bit of thinking, that he'd sent a photo of himself wearing a Santa Claus hat.

Included with the letter was a photograph. It showed only her face and shoulders, and was slightly out of focus, but Jim thought she looked OK.

The letter got Jim very excited. He read it over and over and over again. However, he didn't call her until the following evening. He kept putting it off. Though the letter looked and sounded very promising, he still had nagging doubts and subconscious fears concerning the entire thing.

At last he summoned the nerve to telephone her. They talked briefly, and it was all quite strained and awkward. After a bit they decided to get together the following Friday evening, at a bar on the east side called "The Mystic Umbrella." Jim had never heard of this place, but Rhonda assured him that it was very nice and gave him directions for finding it.

Jim went to sleep that night hopeful, but slightly apprehensive.

Chapter 65

Accompanied by a faint and curious popping noise, Bill materialized in front of the service counter in "Dollars to Donuts." Pauline was leaning against the counter, and jumped up with astonishment at the noise of Bill's unexpected arrival. Bill immediately apologized for startling her, and then apologized for disappearing the month before without warning and without paying rent. He told her that he wouldn't be coming back, and that his room was available. He also gave her a thick wad of cash, saying it should cover his back rent as well as any other expenses he'd caused. Pauline, still a bit shaken by his sudden appearance, merely nodded seriously at everything he said, and stuffed the wad of bills into the pocket of her apron.

Bill then noticed that three members of the Four, namely Bert and the twins, were sitting at one of the curtained booths. He strode over to them.

"Hello, Norman!" he said.

Peter and Paul acknowledged the greeting cheerfully enough, but Bert cut through the smalltalk, immediately asking a question that had been burning a hole in his brain ever since that night at the Cafe, a few weeks before, when they'd last seen Bill.

"So, Bill," he said, "when are you going to take us on a time trip somewhere?"

For several seconds, Bill didn't say anything. He seemed to be thinking, trying to come up with some excuse. He spluttered, "Well, Bert, um, uh..."

"Come on, Bill!" insisted Bert. "We want to go see the Future!"

"Or maybe the past," put in Paul. "I'd love to see the dinosaurs!"

"Or ancient Rome, or the Wild West, or the Civil War!" suggested Peter enthusiastically.

Bill held up his hand to stop their yammerings. "Look guys," he said, "If it were up to me, I'd gladly take you to all those times and places, and many others, too. But you don't have a license, and if I were—"

"A license?" said Bert, incredulous. "A license for what?"

"A license to travel through time!" said Bill. "Look, it's not as simple as you might think. There are a lot of dangers, and one little slip up can cause big problems down the Timeline. If you don't know what you're doing, you can cause serious harm. Therefore, you can't travel through time unless you have a license to do so."

Bert started to say something, but Bill cut him off. "It's just like driving a car. You have to be taught the rules of the road before you go out on the highway; otherwise, you'll cause a big multi-car smash up. And after the crash, if the police found out that you didn't have a license, you'd get in REALLY big trouble."

"OK," said Bert, "how do we get a license?"

Bill sighed, with a slight tinge of disgust. "You have to take an eight month training course, and then pass difficult written and oral examinations. And unfortunately, this training won't be available to you for about seventeen years."

"OK," said Paul, "Then take us forward in time seventeen years, and sign us up for the course!"

Bill smiled ironically. "But I can't do that. Don't you understand? You don't have a license!"

"But it's just one little trip! Who would know?"

"The Time Police, that's who! They watch everything that punches through the Time/Space Continuum! And I could lose my license by transporting a bunch of unlicensed guys across time, even once."

"But you invented the dang thing!" said Bert "Doesn't that give you some special privileges?"

Bill shook his head. "Unfortunately, no."

"So we can't travel through time without a license, and we can't get a license without traveling through time, right?"

"I'm afraid that's correct. You'll just have to wait out the seventeen years."

"Man, this stinks."

"I'm very sorry, Norman," said Bill. "I wish I could change the system. But Time Travel has really taken off, and in order to keep people from destroying history, they had to impose a lot of rules. And it just isn't under my control."

A wave of depression had swept over Peter, Paul, and Bert; they'd been excited by the idea of traveling through time, and the prospect of having to wait seventeen years in order to do so was quite depressing. Why did they have to wait while Bill was zooming back and forth through history? It didn't seem fair to them, and they didn't like it. They sulked.

Bill could see that he wouldn't be able to do anything to cheer them up, and so he quietly slipped away.

Later that evening, Bill was seen in his old room at the Asylum, collecting various things and putting them into a large wooden crate.

Chapter 66

At nineteen minutes past three o'clock on a Friday afternoon in November, Doug entered the lobby of the Harding and Powell Trust & Savings Bank. Under his left arm he held the Atomic Bomb, and in his right hand he held a note. He had wrapped a large pillowcase around the bomb, in order to conceal it. He wore a baseball cap with the brim pulled down low on his forehead, and he kept his eyes fixed on the ground, so that no one would see his face.

He got into line. It being a Friday afternoon, the bank was crowded and the line was long. For several minutes he was the last person in line. The seconds ticked slowly by, and as they did, Doug squirmed. He was, of course, scared out of his wits, and with each tick of the clock he became more and more terrified. He could feel everyone's eyes staring at him, at his curious armload, and at his suspicious countenance. He was just about to abandon the project and quietly leave, when a fat woman with a fat little boy entered the bank and got in line behind him, cutting off his escape.

The line inched forward. Doug trembled. The fat little boy behind him squirmed. He was chewing gum and cracking it loudly, and his mother scolded him several times each minute. Doug became more and more convinced that he should give the whole thing up and leave before something went wrong, but since he was trapped in the looping line of waiting customers, he couldn't exit without causing disruption. He decided to wait until he was first in line and then, instead of walking up to a teller, would he just stroll towards the door and out.

Finally Doug was first in line. He stepped forward, intending to leave. A bell sounded, "BING." It was the "Teller Available" bell of the teller just before him. Doug froze, looking at the teller. The teller looked at him impatiently. The little boy behind him popped his gum and squeaked "GO! You're next!"

Doug felt as if he'd lost control of his life. It seemed to him that, even though his brain wanted him to run, his body was forcing him to go through with the plan. It was as if he were a character in a videogame. Someone else was playing the game, and by moving the joystick this way or that, was controlling his actions. He felt an overwhelming desire to abandon this crazy project and get away, to escape down the street and into the nearby subway tunnels. But the man with the joystick overruled him.

Doug's brain was screaming at him not to do it, but Doug's body approached the teller and handed her this note:

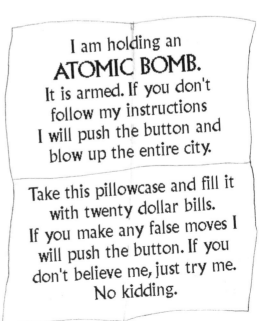

I am holding an **ATOMIC BOMB.** It is armed. If you don't follow my instructions I will push the button and blow up the entire city.

Take this pillowcase and fill it with twenty dollar bills. If you make any false moves I will push the button. If you don't believe me, just try me. No kidding.

As the teller (in rather great astonishment) read the note, Doug took the pillowcase off of the bomb. He put the pillowcase down in front of the teller and set the bomb up on the counter in plain sight. Then he poised his index finger in front of the big red button, ready to press it, and waited.

The crowd in the bank had by this time noticed the bomb, and a quiet panic swept through them as they acknowledged the implications of what they were seeing. Several people immediately bolted for the door, and went running off down the street. Several others edged towards the door, keen to get away but also realizing that they couldn't possibly get far enough away quickly enough to save themselves. Still others thought they should try to get away but were too interested in watching the events unfold to make a run for it. Finally, there were those who couldn't rationalize their behavior at all, and simply stood there, transfixed.

The teller was stuffing cash into the pillowcase with all the alacrity she could muster.

Doug was attempting to stay calm, and even though things were going comparatively smoothly, he was so paranoid that he was convinced that things were one step from disaster. With the pillowcase only two thirds full, he screamed "That's enough! Give it to me!"

The teller, with her eyes bulging and her mouth gaping, complied.

Doug grabbed at the bag with his left hand, and then attempted to wrestle the bomb off of the counter with his right. All he had to do was get the bomb down, walk swiftly out of the bank, get to the subway entrance, and become lost in the anonymity of the underground. But he botched it.

He was off balance and trembling with terror. The swinging pillowcase combined with the act of manhandling a heavy object down from a fairly high location resulted in disaster. The bomb tipped forward and fell heavily against his chest. In the frozen silence of the bank lobby, the click of the big red button being pressed resounded like a curse word spoken during a church service prayer. The various lights on the front panel of the bomb lit up. The big red digital counter underneath the words "SECONDS UNTIL DETONATION" suddenly displayed the number "60," which after a second changed to "59," then to "58."

Doug gripped the bomb with both hands, closed his eyes, and whispered "no." The pillowcase of money fell to the floor with a quiet rustle, like leaves blowing across concrete on a cool autumn afternoon.

Now the crowd really did panic. Many of them realized the futility of attempting to run, but ran nonetheless, in blind terror. Several sat down on the floor, with vacant, horrified expressions etched across their faces. The little boy with the gum began to cry, and his mother said, over and over again, "This can't be happening, this just can't be happening."

Doug, however, simply stood there. He was frozen in place, trying to imagine what it would be like to be vaporized by the impending atomic blast. He remembered that people who were about to die always had their lives flash before them, and he thought back over the events that had led him to this fateful moment.

When the counter read "48," an alarm started ringing in the lobby of the bank, and several of the employees jumped up from their hiding places behind the counter and ran for the door.

When the counter read "27," the fat woman wailed, "Well, I'll be damned if I'm going to spend my last few seconds in a BANK!" And she grabbed her little boy by the wrist and dragged him out the door.

When the counter read "11," Doug took off his cap and looked up at the few remaining bank patrons, who stood around like zombies or sprawled like exhausted children on the floor. "I'm sorry," said Doug, "I didn't mean for this to happen." He looked down at the bomb, and the counter now read "7." He wanted to explain himself and his actions, but he couldn't figure out what to say, and his voice trailed off. "It's just that, well..."

The counter ticked off the final seconds. "3"..."2"..."1"..."0."

The counter stopped at zero.

Nothing happened.

Doug looked at the bomb, all at once realizing that it was a dud and that he might still get away with his robbery after all. He relaxed his grip on the bomb, and it fell to the floor with a loud crash. Then he grabbed the pillowcase and ran for the door. By the time he reached it,

two of the bank customers had come to their senses and they attempted to grab him, but he wrestled free and escaped.

Outside, however, several police cars had arrived. Doug ran for the subway, but he didn't make it. Guns flashed out of holsters, shouted threats lashed across the concrete, warning shots echoed up and down the street, and running boots clattered on the pavement.

Half crazy with fear, Doug stopped, and again dropped the pillowcase. This time, it fell open. Four twenty dollar bills flew out, and were blown across the street by the wind.

Chapter 67

It took another 14 minutes for the Bomb Squad to arrive. When they did, they handled the Atomic Bomb very carefully, believing that it was still highly dangerous even though it hadn't exploded. It may have been a dud, but it still had to be handled with care and respect. They also felt there was a slim chance that it might still explode.

With great delicacy, they removed the bomb from the bank and took it back to the Crime Lab.

There, with extreme care, they removed the numerous bolts from the bomb casing.

When they saw what was inside, or more accurately what *wasn't* inside, their apprehension turned to anger.

"This ain't no bomb!" shouted a demolitions expert. "This box is no more harmful than a toaster!"

"A phony bomb," said another. "We were all stressed out over a phony bomb."

A third was laughing. "But you gotta admit, it sure fooled a lot of people!"

One of the arresting officers looked concerned. "If it wasn't a real bomb, then we can't charge him with assault with a deadly weapon, or possession of nuclear armaments, or terrorism, or—"

"It doesn't matter," interrupted one of the other police officers. "It doesn't have to be a real weapon if the victims *think* it's a real weapon. It's still assault. Plus, he did succeed in stealing money from the bank, which means he still committed a robbery, even though he didn't get very far with the loot. So, no problem. We got the witnesses, we got the bank monitor tapes, we got the alleged 'weapon'—it's an open and shut case. Hardly any point in having a trial."

"Yeah, I guess you're right," admitted the officer who had been concerned. "You wanna go get some coffee and donuts?"

"Yeah, sounds good to me." And they left the Crime Lab.

Chapter 68

"I just can't believe it was Doug," said Dave. "That goofus in the elevator. I'd never have figured he'd try something like that."

The Four sat in a curtained booth at "Dollars to Donuts," where they'd just finished reading the newspaper account of Doug's nuclear holdup.

"I can't believe it was our bomb," said Peter.

"Poor guy'll probably get twenty years in prison," said Paul.

"Man, that would be tough," said Bert.

"Oh, jail probably won't be so hard on him," said Dave.

"Are you kidding?" asked Bert, incredulous. "It would stink!"

"Well, think about it," explained Dave. "That guy spent all of his free time hanging around in an elevator. He's obviously not too concerned about being cooped up in a small space for long stretches of time."

Bert shrugged. "I guess not, but I still feel sorry for him."

"All I know," said Paul, "is that he won't be clogging up the elevator anymore, and I for one am glad about that."

They tossed this topic around for a while longer, and then they played Icehouse. Dave used some of the new strategies he'd learned from The Emperor and Doctor Cool, and utterly trounced Bert, Peter, and Paul.

Chapter 69

Jim knew from the moment he saw Rhonda that the whole thing was a mistake. It was non-love at first sight.

She was sitting at a small table near the back of the bar. The table looked very small indeed because Rhonda looked so big. She wasn't exactly fat (though she was certainly a bit overweight) she was just big. She was tall and had a large frame, broad shoulders, and big, muscular arms. Jim, who was neither tall nor heavyset, felt daunted and puny when he looked at Rhonda. This was also a bit of a surprise for him. He'd been fearful about the adjective "tremendous" but had forgotten about this concern after looking at the photo she'd sent. The portrait-style photograph had completely failed to convey her large size, and Jim was therefore rather shocked by it.

Jim stood a few feet back from the table looking at her, wondering if he had any chance of escape, if he could move on past the table without stopping, acting as if he were someone else, casually wandering towards the door and into the safety and freedom of the night air. However, he hesitated too long.

Rhonda looked at him and smiled. "Jim! Hello!"

Jim faked a smile. "Hi! You must be Rhonda!"

"Yep! Have a seat! I've already ordered some appetizers."

Jim frantically tried to think of some way of getting out of all of this, but was unable to. He stood there, awkwardly looking at Rhonda, who smiled back at him unceasingly. At last he resigned himself to the ordeal, and slumped into the chair.

"I ordered mozzarella sticks and chicken wings," said Rhonda. "They should arrive any minute."

"Oh good," said Jim with actual enthusiasm, since he very much liked both chicken wings and mozzarella sticks.

Another thing that surprised and disturbed Jim was her hair. The Rhonda in the photo had straight, smooth hair, which seemed fairly long and looked very nice. The Rhonda in person had short, permed, very curly hair, which Jim disliked intensely.

"Did you have any trouble finding the place?" asked Rhonda.

"No, no trouble at all," said Jim.

Jim was embarrassed by the long stretches of silence, even though Rhonda continued to smile at Jim and seemed almost contented. Jim wondered what Rhonda was thinking.

The waitress appeared, set the appetizers on the table, asked if they wished to order drinks, wrote down their orders, and vanished. Jim noticed that the waitress was very attractive, and as she scurried away he wished wistfully that he was having this blind date with her instead. Rhonda had ordered a beer, but Jim, who wasn't much of a drinker, had ordered a Coke. He immediately wished that he too had ordered a beer; it was going to be a long meal.

They munched mozzarella sticks and chicken wings. Rhonda attempted to start conversation on several topics: music, movies, hobbies. Her interests struck Jim as commonplace and dull, and the conversations quickly fell apart.

Rhonda's face was caked with makeup. She'd been wearing makeup in the photo, but not as much and not as thickly applied. It wasn't so very noticeable in the picture, but in real life, it looked ghastly. Her lips were bright red, glossy, and rather plastic looking. Her eyelids were blue. Pink smudges incrusted her cheeks. Jim found all of this ugly and revolting. He hated makeup. He thought it looked stupid and unnatural. He thought Rhonda looked more like a Barbie doll than an actual person. Why were her eyelids blue? Blue isn't a normal color for eyelids.

Rhonda appeared to be searching for some topic of conversation to bring up. At last she broke the silence. "Have you got your Christmas shopping done yet?"

What Jim thought was "Good Lord, it's the last week of November! Who gets their Christmas shopping done this early?"

What Jim said was "No, not yet. It's kind of early, isn't it?"

Rhonda said, "Oh, I guess, but I always like to get my Christmas shopping done early. I hate dealing with the crowds at the mall."

Jim couldn't think of anything to say to this, particularly because he thought that anyone who finished their Christmas shopping a month in advance was goofy. Silence again dominated their conversation.

The waitress reappeared, with the beer and the Coke. She asked if they were ready to order their entrees.

Jim's single goal was to find a way of ending the ordeal as quickly and painlessly as possible. He said, "Gee, I don't know. I wasn't really all that hungry, and the appetizers kind of filled me up."

Rhonda wouldn't go for it, though. She clucked over Jim's lack of appetite, but it didn't inhibit her own. "Well, I'm going to have the grilled turkey and Swiss. Are you sure you don't want anything, Jim?"

Jim had been lying about not being very hungry, but he couldn't change his story too drastically. "Oh, OK, I guess I'll have an order of fries."

The awkward minutes crawled by. Rhonda had realized by now that the whole thing was collapsing and she was attempting to shore it up with a new round of conversation starters. These of course did no good. Jim was reminded of the hours he spent in church as a kid, listening to endless sermons, desperately impatient for liberation and freedom, but bound by etiquette and a stern mother to sit still and to act calm and serene.

The waitress finally arrived with their food, and the process of eating took the attention off of the lack of conversation.

And the time finally came when the end was in sight. The waitress brought the check, and Jim paid it. Then, acting quickly lest his parole be denied, he stood up and said to Rhonda, "Well. This was very nice. I'll call you next week, OK?"

Rhonda looked blankly at Jim. "OK," she said. Then it looked like she might say something else, so Jim quickly said "OK! Then I guess I'll see you later." And he turned his back on her and strolled, as quickly and yet as casually as he could, toward the front door. As he exited, he looked back and saw that Rhonda was still sitting at the table. She had her elbow on the table and was holding her head up with her right hand, her palm pressed against her forehead.

On returning home, Jim located and threw away Rhonda's photo, letter, and phone number. He never intended to call her again. Then he locked himself into his closet, put a fresh sheet of paper into his typewriter, and began to write a story.

He worked on it until 2:30 in the morning.

It was called "Wishing Well."

Chapter 70

"WISHING WELL"
By James L. Ruckel

William Kennington was looking for love. He had been involved with someone for a span of several years, and when that relationship suddenly ended, he found himself unable to start a new one. The landscape of his social arena had changed dramatically during the time in which he'd been unavailable. Once he'd known many single women, he now discovered that they were all married or seriously involved with others. So for many months he struggled, with very little success, to meet someone who was single, whom he found interesting, and who also found him interesting.

He tried all the usual methods. He became very socially active, going to many parties and gatherings. He went to singles bars and nightclubs. He tried to get his friends, neighbors, relatives, and co-workers to introduce him to people. He had a few dates, but none he found very worthwhile.

After many failures he began to get desperate. He responded to a number of "personal" ads in the newspaper, and after a while, he placed his own. He called up several of those 976 "party-line" phone numbers. He joined a dating service. Still nothing worked.

One day it came into his head that Fate was working against him. In order to find out why, William sought out the services of a psychic. She read his palm and told him that he was going to get married and would have a very strong, long term relationship.

"How soon?" asked William.

"You will also have three children," said the palm reader.

"What will my wife's name be?" asked William.

"I'm not sure," said the psychic. "It's hard to tell."

"I don't get this," said William. "You can tell my future, and you can tell me something specific like how many children I will have, but you can't give me any actual, useful data?"

"Well—"

"If you know I'm going to get married, why can't you tell me the woman's name so that I can go meet her and get on with things?"

"I'm afraid it doesn't work like that—"

"What's the use of a trade like fortune telling if you can't give me information that I can actually use? If you know I'm going to get married, then you should be able to tell me the name, address, and telephone number of the woman I'll eventually marry!"

"If I could do that, do you think I'd be working out of a 2-bit joint like this?"

"I guess not." William grabbed his hat and left.

He tried several other psychics, including a couple of tarot card readers, a tea leaf reader, an old man who supposedly saw visions of the future in his dreams, and a young Italian woman with a fortune teller's act so corny that she actually employed a big crystal ball. But they all gave him conflicting predictions, none of which held up to his ruthless scientific analysis.

One day, William Kennington was strolling through the park, glumly considering his failed romantic efforts. He passed a small wishing well, one he'd passed many times before without a moment's thought. This time he paused, and looked down at the layer of pennies, nickels, dimes, and quarters that shimmered below the surface of the still water.

Suddenly gripped by an absurd impulse, William pulled out the half dollar coin which he habitually carried as a good luck piece. Wishing to meet the girl of his dreams, he tossed it in. It sank to the bottom with a loud plop.

And that very day, William Kennington met a wonderful girl named Elizabeth Zinnimann in the Smith Brother's Supermarket. He was carrying an armload of groceries, and she ran over his foot with a grocery cart. It started as a bizarre accident, but apologies gave way to casual conversation and eventually to an exchange of phone numbers.

They dated for four months and then she moved into his apartment. They were perfect for each other, and were very deeply in love. They even started making plans for marriage. William Kennington became the happiest man in the world, and every time he passed by the wishing well, he thanked his lucky stars for granting his wish.

One day William Kennington was walking by the wishing well and noticed that it was being emptied out. Two men were standing in the water, scooping up the coins with buckets, and handing them to men at the top, who dumped the coins into a big vat on a truck. William wandered over to the workmen.

"What happens to the coins when they're removed?" William asked.

"They're given to charity," grunted a workman.

William wandered off, but a bigger question burned in his brain. "What happens," he wondered, "if a wish gets granted, and then, later on, the coin that was wished upon gets removed from the wishing well? Does removal of the coins imply cancellation of the wishes as well?"

As he thought this, William felt a sudden twinge of pain and loss that he could not account for. Then he brushed off his questions. "After all," he thought, "everyone knows wishing wells don't really grant wishes. Why, I myself tossed in a whole half dollar once, and my wish didn't come true."

William wandered glumly back to his lonely apartment. He perused the newspaper's personal ads, but found none worth responding to. He spent the whole evening feeling sorry for himself, and that night he slept a very restless sleep.

Chapter 71

Dave opened his eyes.

He was somewhere dark, in the middle of the night. He was in a chilly room, under a thick, warm blanket. The Martian Princess was curled up next to him. And he could see something, or someone, in the corner.

He remembered that her name was Alyson. At least that was what the Princess had told him, though he wondered how she had found out.

Alyson was sitting in a rocking chair, reading a book. She rocked slowly, back and forth. It was very difficult to see her; it was like trying to get a good look at the spots that you see in front of your eyes after someone has taken a flash photo of you. Her form was indistinct and elusive. The chair didn't rest on the floor, but hovered in the air. Alyson constantly looked down at her book; her head never seemed to move.

Dave watched her for a long time, for perhaps half an hour. Every few minutes, she turned a page, but she didn't take her eyes off the book. Dave never moved, never stirred. He just lay there, watching.

Then, she became even harder to discern, even fainter than before, and Dave squinted and strained to see her. And finally, she faded altogether.

Dave lay awake for another half hour, wondering and thinking. He caressed the woman beside him and she stirred, but did not wake.

After he went back to sleep, Dave had a dream. He dreamt he was working at a concession stand in a movie theater. The strange thing was that the refreshments were in vending machines, located behind the concession counter. Dave was acting as an unnecessary liaison between the customers and the machines. When, for example, a patron requested Milk Duds, Dave would take the money, feed the bills into an automatic changer, put the coins into the candy dispensing machine, pull the lever for Milk Duds, and finally hand the box that fell out of the machine to the customer. As instructed by the movie theater management, Dave was charging a dollar sixty for a box of Milk Duds, even though it only cost fifty cents to buy them from the machine. The real prices were marked on the vending machines, and were clearly visible to the customers, who frequently became enraged at the blatant mark up. Each customer seemed more angry about the situation than the previous one had been, and they began to threaten Dave with physical violence. They yelled loudly, and brandished grisly looking weapons, such as huge, rusty iron axes and clubs with pointy metal spikes. Finally Dave hid under the counter. The customers became even more angry at the lack of service, and shouted and pounded on the counter with baseball bats and sledge hammers.

Then it was morning, and Dave awoke with a throbbing headache.

Chapter 72

Jim heard the phone ring, but he didn't get up to answer it.

It rang twice. Then, after a short delay, Jim heard Suzanne yelling "Jim! It's for you!"

Jim had been lying in bed, lonely and depressed and feeling sorry for himself. But now, someone wanted to talk to him, and he jumped up excitedly and grabbed the receiver.

"Hello?"

"Hi, Jim!"

A cheerful voice. Jennifer's.

Jim was silent. After several seconds, Jennifer said, "Hello?"

"Hello, Jennifer." Jim sounded sad and rundown, and that was how he felt. He'd already been feeling blue, and a call from his ex-girlfriend wasn't something he needed at this time. It was like hitting a skull fracture patient in the head by suddenly opening a door in his path.

Jennifer attempted to recompose her cheerful aspect. "How are you doing, Jim? It's been a long time."

Jim sighed. "I'm doing OK. How are you?"

"Oh, I'm fine," said Jennifer.

Then came a lull.

Jennifer said, "So, how's work?"

Jim sighed. "Work's about the same as always. How's your job?"

"Mmm, it's OK. We got a new color copier, which is pretty neat."

Jim grunted. Another lull ensued.

Jennifer struggled to keep the conversation going. "So," she said "You're doing OK?"

Jim shrugged, and then realized that this answer wouldn't work over the phone. He said, "Yeah, I'm OK."

Silence. Jim and Jennifer listened to each other breathe.

Jennifer said, "I wish we could still be friends, Jim."

Jim didn't say anything.

After another lapse of silence, Jennifer said, "So, have you written anything new?"

Jim was on the verge of crying. He was choked up, and knew that he wouldn't be able to talk much longer. "Um," he said, "I kind of have to go now."

Now Jennifer sighed. "OK, Jim. Um, I'll talk to you later, OK?"

"Yeah, OK, goodbye," said Jim. He hung up the phone, and began silently weeping.

Chapter 73

The weeks before Christmas slipped away day by day as crowds of happy shoppers descended upon the City's numerous malls and retail outlets. They came, they saw, they purchased.

At last, Christmas day itself arrived. Everywhere in the City people met with good cheer and happy tidings, making reality out of the fantasies depicted in TV specials, on Christmas cards, and in Norman Rockwell paintings. Turkeys were carved. Carols were sung. Gifts were exchanged. And greedy children wished for more.

Christmas even came to the Federal Penitentiary, located a few miles to the north of the City, in which Doug had been incarcerated for the crimes of Bank Robbery and Nuclear Terrorism.

Doug stood leaning against the wall of his cell. He was enjoying the day off. Christmas was a day of rest for the inmates. On most days, they labored in the prison shops, making clothes, brushes, and license plates, but the shops were closed today because of the holiday.

Doug was having a rather hard time adjusting to the new working routine, and enjoyed the freedom of his tiny cell. The cell was in many ways similar to his elevator, and he found his time there almost enjoyable.

The midday meal in the prison cafeteria had been far better than usual. Roast turkey, cranberry sauce, mashed potatoes with thick, tasty gravy, fluffy dinner rolls with real butter, hot coffee, and even steaming apple pie, served with a scoop of vanilla ice cream on top! For the first time since his imprisonment, Doug had eaten everything on his tray.

That evening, the prisoners entertained themselves with a variety show. The cast sang many of the standard Christmas carols, along with a couple of original compositions by inmates. The cast also performed a scene from *A Christmas Carol*, by Charles Dickens. Finally, a prisoner dressed as Santa Claus appeared, and handed out candy canes and bars of chocolate to the prisoners in the audience.

Later, leaning against the wall in his cell, Doug slowly ate his chocolate bar. "Prison ain't so bad," he thought to himself.

Chapter 74

You could hear the noise from the Android Sisters' New Year's Eve Party as soon as the elevator doors opened on the fourth floor of their apartment building.

Each year, the Android Sisters held exactly one party, and it was always big. Last year it had been a Halloween party. This year they'd selected New Year's Eve.

The apartment was crowded. The Androids had given out an open invitation, and practically everyone had accepted it.

All of the Asylum inmates were there. Suzanne and Lynda had both brought their current boyfriends, and Torrence had of course brought Maria. Jim and Pauline, however, had come stag. Although Pauline didn't care, this bothered Jim a great deal. It had been years since he'd been alone on New Year's Eve.

Also in attendance was Wanda, the new inmate of the Asylum. She had just finished moving into Bill's old room in the basement. She was short and thin, with curly brown hair. Her main creative output was T-shirts; she did custom screening as well as all manner of tie-dyed shirts.

And even Bill was there, though he only stayed a few minutes. He popped in, chatted with a few specific people, and then disappeared.

Needless to say, the Four were there, and they had dressed for the occasion.

Bert was dressed as the outgoing old year: he wore a ridiculous long white beard, and carried a big sickle. Over his long white robe he had draped a Miss America style banner with the old year imprinted on it. He made a big show of hobbling slowly around, and leaning on his sickle for support.

Peter was dressed as the incoming new year. A huge white diaper and a banner bearing the new year's date were his sole adornments. Sometimes he crawled around on the floor, but other times, feeling ridiculous, he stood up and acted like a normal, albeit oddly dressed, person.

Paul was dressed as the new year as it would be a couple of months hence: an obnoxious, pimply youth. He wore ripped up jeans and a dirty T-shirt under his date emblazoned banner. He had a sling shot in his back pocket and a skateboard under his arm. He teased the girls, cracked his bubble gum loudly and frequently, and fidgeted constantly.

Dave was dressed as the new year in the prime of its life, about nine months in the future. He wore a smart looking business suit under the obligatory year banner and carried a briefcase in one hand and a copy of the Wall Street Journal in the other. He talked seriously about the stock market and other business matters.

And along with these were gathered many other people, a wide assortment: close friends, distant friends, friends of friends, and even a couple of complete strangers. Music blared and conversations droned. Refreshments were consumed.

The Android Sisters, as the hostesses, looked stunning in their matching, shimmering white evening gowns. Since the party was being catered, they were able to spend all of their time socializing with their guests.

At ten o'clock, the Martian Princess quietly slipped through the door. She located Dave and silently stood behind him until he noticed her.

When he did, he kissed her and said "Hi!"

"Hello," she whispered.

"I see you found the place," said Dave. "Check out our costumes, aren't they great!"

The Princess gazed around, but didn't say anything.

"There are refreshments and stuff over there," said Dave, pointing at a table.

The Princess wandered off in the indicated direction, and poured herself a glass of punch. She then sat down on the floor in the corner, near where Mr. Bean, the manager of the Saturn Cafe, stood talking to his small wife.

Jim also sat nearby. He was in a melancholy mood. At times during the party, he'd put on his best face and act social, trying to get some kind of conversation going with one or another of the women he didn't know; but at other times, he just sat quietly, drinking punch from a clear plastic cup and feeling sorry for himself.

At ten twenty five, Dave knelt down next to the Princess, who had not stirred from the spot in the corner. He looked at her seriously. "Are you OK?"

The Princess shrugged. "I'm just in an anti-social mood."

Dave sagged. "Do you want to leave? We could go somewhere else."

The Princess said, "I don't want to drag you away if you're having fun."

"No, it's OK, I can leave. Do you want to go?"

The Princess shrugged, but then nodded.

"OK," said Dave, "Let's get out of here." With that, they headed for the door, and disappeared into the chilly winter night.

Bert noticed their departure, and seethed. He told the others. They felt hurt and angry, and stood together in a huddle, whispering to each other.

"It doesn't really matter," said Peter, "his costume was the least interesting one."

"It *does* matter," insisted Paul. "Without his costume, mine's not as good. The baby and the old man are standards, but the adolescent doesn't really work without the grown-up."

"Is this the way it's going to be?" asked Bert. "We've been seeing less and less of Dave. He never has time for us anymore, because of his 'Princess.' Soon they're gonna start calling us 'The Three.' "

They felt glum. But after a bit, they resumed their antics and more or less forgot about Dave.

At eleven thirty, Jim managed to get a conversation going with an attractive woman named Jill. They chatted, and the chemistry seemed to be working OK. He asked if she wanted something to drink, and then went off to get two cups of punch. He returned, and they sat down on the edge of a couch to drink punch and talk.

At eleven fifty three, someone turned on the television and the crowd became aware of the approaching moment of celebration.

At eleven fifty seven, Jill said "Oop! It's almost midnight!" She finished off her punch in one big swallow, stood up and walked off, calling back over her shoulder "I'll be back!"

Jim sat waiting impatiently. He'd become very agitated by Jill's departure, and longed for her timely return. As their conversation had progressed, he'd been hopeful that something might grow out of it. He desperately wanted to be with Jill at midnight, since at that special moment, everyone is supposed to kiss the one they love. Although they barely knew each other, Jim imagined that their inhibitions might drop away in the spirit of the moment, and that he and Jill might join lips, thus starting off a relationship in a wonderful, magic way.

At eleven fifty nine and forty seconds, Jim could wait no longer, and went off to find Jill. He pushed through the crowd, which was beginning to chant the seconds as they ticked away.

At eleven fifty nine and fifty five seconds, Jim found Jill. She was standing in the kitchen, laughing, with her arms around a tall blond man.

At midnight, the crowd erupted. They hugged and shouted and cheered and kissed and laughed and screamed and frolicked. Paul, as the baby new year, put on a big show of chasing Bert, the old man, out of the apartment. Jill and her tall blond man engaged in a long, passionate kiss.

And Jim stood alone, still and silent, in the doorway of the kitchen.

At ten minutes after midnight, Jim quietly left the party. He walked out into the cold winter night, and on into the Empty City. The noise of the party echoed in his brain.

Chapter 75

Dave had a dream.

In the dream, he was a Spaceman. He had landed on Mars. He'd left his rocket ship out on a windswept Martian desert, and was walking across the red sand dunes towards a Martian City. He had seen the City from orbit, and had brought his ship down towards it, down to the place where the City stretched out from the intersections of three large canals, down onto the red Martian desert, just a mile or so away from the outskirts of the City.

The City stretched out low on the horizon. Its buildings were of ancient stone, built thousands of years ago and yet unchanged. The houses were of simple, yet elegant architecture: large geometric shapes, huge stone spheres, obelisks, and pyramids, pyramids tall and narrow and short and squat, three sided, four sided, five sided pyramids.

As Dave grew near, a canal sliced across his path, and he followed it into the City Square. Cold blue water stirred quietly in the long canal, and presently a boat came into view, a long graceful boat, with huge, colorful sails. And now he saw the Martians.

They wore simple, solid colored clothes, long and loose, flowing like gowns, fluttering softly in the gentle Martian breeze. The sunlight shown upon their long, rich red hair, and their emerald green eyes looked up at Dave, warm and friendly.

Dave entered the City. All around were the ancient Martian buildings, the stone spheres and pyramids, all with windows of beautiful colored crystal. At the heart of the City was a wide square mall, set about here and there with bronze sculptures and crystal pillars and small fountains in which cool, clear blue water danced and burbled. And all around him were the Martians, strolling about, moving in and out of their ancient stone buildings, talking and laughing in musical voices.

In one corner of the City Square, Dave saw Martians gathered around small, round tables, carved of stone, playing a game. The playing pieces were little pyramids, made of colored crystals.

In another corner was a sort of marketplace, where Martians had gathered to buy and sell various things. Dave strolled among the merchants, but could make little sense of the wares being offered. One table was strewn with thin metal rods of different colors that were either cool or quite warm to the touch. At another booth, a Martian woman offered, among many other strange things, a purple metal sphere with small holes in it, through which a fragrant mist was occasionally released. He also saw odd stone heptahedrons, a variety of white cubic vessels containing strange green sponge-like substances, and a large number of polished metal slabs with raised symbols set upon them. When these symbols were touched, the slab would speak, in that musical language of the Martians.

Martian money seemed to consist entirely of three sided gold coins, but bartering was also quite welcome in the market, and one of the merchants finally persuaded him to trade his laser pistol for a strange rock-like object, made of metal, which emitted a pleasing jingling sort of sound when shaken.

Just after this, a stir went through the crowd, and looking up, Dave saw a strange vehicle approaching from the rust colored desert beyond the City. It was a walking machine, a gleaming, insect-like metal tripod that strode quickly across the hot deserts of Mars. Mounted on the tripod's long articulated legs was a sort of carriage, and when the tripod stopped at last in the center of the square, several Martians descended from this carriage and moved among the crowd. One of them particularly caught his eye.

She wore a flowing green gown, and her hair, though of the same rich red color as all of the other Martians, was far longer than that of any other Martian he had seen. It flowed back from her head down to her ankles, nearly dragging on the ground as she walked through the City Square.

"Who is that?" Dave said aloud, not really intending to.

"The Empress, of course," said a tall Martian nearby, speaking to him for the first time in his own language.

Dave awoke at this point to the jarring blare of his alarm clock, and found himself back on Earth.

Chapter 76

Jim went over to the shopping center. It being the first week in January, the mall was now a quiet, sleepy place. The frantic weeks of sales leading up to Christmas were over, and the casual days of cleanup and recovery had mostly passed.

Very few people were out shopping this evening, but even so, Jim was hanging around in hopes of meeting someone. It was a new scheme of his.

Jim had been without a love life for the past four months and was rather sick of it. His various attempts at meeting someone he found attractive and interesting and who found him attractive and interesting had all been failures.

He had tried going to bars, the classic way for people to meet, but had hated it. He wasn't much of a drinker, and the atmosphere was always wrong. Too strained, too sleazy. He always felt awkward and uncomfortable, and could never bring himself to hang around for very long. Further, he never felt that he'd meet anyone worth bothering with at a pickup joint. He wanted to meet someone sincere and intelligent, and who, most of all, wanted a long term relationship, and not just a one night stand. It was of course possible that the woman of his dreams was in fact at such a place, hating it every bit as much as Jim, and Jim realized this... but he couldn't bring himself to wait around and see.

He'd tried playing the personals game, but that had been a disaster so far. Nevertheless, he continued researching the ads every week.

He had looked up every old friend and acquaintance he had, but found no one who wasn't either uninterested, uninteresting to him, or unavailable.

He'd asked his various friends to help him out, to introduce him to anyone they knew who they thought he might like and have a chance with, but nothing had come of it.

Then one night, after a conversation with his housemate Pauline, he'd devised a new plan.

The conversation in question had occurred late one night in the kitchen of the Asylum. Earlier that evening, Jim had tried visiting a couple of bars but had ending up just aimlessly wandering the streets. Finally, around midnight, he'd gone home, where he'd found Pauline sitting on the floor in front of the stove.

"What are you doing?" asked Jim.

Pauline yawned. "Well, the stove's kind of screwy, you know. I think its thermostat is shot. Sometimes it gets way too hot." She got up on her knees, cracked the oven door open, and peered in. "I'm baking some chocolate chip cookies. If you just let them cook for the normal time, they burn. You've gotta keep an eye on them, and get them out of there as soon as they're ready."

Jim sat down at the kitchen table, ready to mooch cookies when they were done. He sighed heavily.

Pauline looked at him with a motherly sort of expression. "How you doing, Jim? You look depressed."

"Well, it's just, you know how it is. My love life needs some help, that's all."

Pauline nodded sadly. She took another peek at her cookies, and concluded they were done. As she scraped cookies off of the sheet with a big spatula, Jim poured two tall glasses of fresh, cold milk.

They sat at the table to enjoy the classic treat, cookies and milk. Pauline said, "Well, Jim, let me give you some advice. The key to meeting someone is to look like you aren't looking. Even if you're single and on the prowl, you will often get scared off if you meet someone who looks really desperate. Of course, this isn't easy. If you are looking, it's hard to act like you aren't looking and make any progress at looking. It's a hard line to walk. You have to seem available without looking desperate."

"Any suggestions on how?" asked Jim, somewhat cynically.

"Well, I've found that the best way of meeting guys is to bump into them in public places. I don't actually mean physically bumping into them, I mean seeing someone and finding a way of striking up a conversation.

"So, for example, if you're in the grocery store and you see a nice looking girl, find an excuse for doing shopping right near where she's doing shopping. Then, strike up a conversation. The grocery store is loaded with conversation starters. Say 'Excuse me, but do you know if these chicken pot pies are any good?' or 'Oh, don't buy Minute Maid orange juice, the Tropicana is much better.' Then, arrange things so that you get into line right behind her. Keep the conversation going. Maybe you can even help her carry her groceries. Follow through with a casual inquiry as to her name, and then ask for her phone number.

"It's a good way of meeting people because it's not as stilted as, like, going to a singles bar. It makes it seem like it's Fate, or something. The grocery store is particularly good because you can learn a lot about your target by casual examination of the food she's buying. Just remember to check out her hand. If you see a wedding ring, it's time to move on."

Jim felt as though he was being told the secret of life from a guru in the Himalayas. He nodded gravely as he listened to the sage's words of advice and consumed the sage's chocolate chip cookies.

After she'd finished, Pauline got up, put the remaining cookies into a chipped pottery cookie jar, and piled the dishes up in the sink. As she did this, neither she nor Jim said anything, each keeping their thoughts private. Finally, Pauline picked up the cookie jar and wandered off. "Well," she said as she walked down the hallway, "I hope that helps. Goodnight."

"Goodnight," said Jim. He had stayed at the table for a long time, slowly drinking the rest of his milk and thinking about the things Pauline had said.

Over the days that followed, Jim had done a great deal of grocery shopping. Even so, he had failed to make any contacts. He then decided to broaden his scope, and had gone to the bigger marketplace of the shopping center.

This evening, the mall was quiet. Jim wished he'd had Pauline's wisdom a month ago, when the stores were crowded. Jim wandered through the record store, but saw only a rather hideous punk rocker. He went through several clothing stores, but the only women he saw there were far too fashion conscious for his taste. He saw only men in the stereo and appliances store, and the only person in the candy store was a pleasant little gray-haired lady who reminded Jim of his grandmother. There, he bought some fudge.

And finally, he came to the bookstore.

Standing at one of the fiction racks in the bookstore was an attractive young woman. She had round wire-rimmed glasses, large dangly earrings, and a small mole on the left side of her nose. Her hair seemed long but was wound up in a tight braid which was bobbypinned to her skull in a bun. She was wearing a full, gray woolen skirt and a white sweater over a tie-dyed shirt. Though her clothes were rather shapeless, she seemed to have a slim, shapely body. She stood there, reading a book.

Jim strolled as casually as he could up and down the aisles on either side of the one in which the woman stood reading. He was excited. She was attractive and intelligent! He braced himself to wander near her, but then lost his nerve and went back to the magazine racks.

He stood there, staring at magazines he didn't care at all about. He was keenly aware of the present. He felt that he had one chance, that if he didn't make some kind of move, she'd disappear and he'd never see her again.

He wandered around the aisles again, and this time managed to walk down the one in which she stood. She was blocking the way, and as he approached, she rotated to give him room to pass. He hesitated, and then spoke, trying not to sound too nervous.

"What are you reading?" he said.

She looked up at him and laughed, and waved her hand to dismiss his question. "You've never heard of him," she said.

"Oh, come on, try me," said Jim.

She closed the book and held it up for him to see. It was a collection of short stories by Donald Barthelme called *Sixty Stories*.

Jim was very surprised. "Barthelme!" he said. "I love his stuff!" This was true. Barthelme was a writer of abstract fiction whom Jim greatly admired. His nervousness washed away.

The woman looked at him skeptically. "Really?" she asked. "I thought he was fairly obscure."

"Maybe he is," said Jim, "But I really admire his work. The first thing I ever read by him was 'Porcupines at the University,' and it really blew my mind. You see, I'm a writer myself, and when I discovered his stuff, it opened up a whole new world for me."

Now the woman was interested. "Really?" she asked. "Have you gotten much published?"

Jim looked sheepish. "Well, no, not really. One story I did was printed in a little magazine called *The Midnight Xerox*. But I haven't tried very hard to get my stuff published. I'm still, you know, learning my craft."

"Hmm," said the woman.

In the brief lull that followed, Jim remembered Pauline's advice and snuck a peek at her hands. No rings at all. Good! But then the silence expanded and became awkward, and Jim feared the encounter might flop. He suddenly spoke up, sounding a bit too panicky, "Would you like to read some of my stuff?"

This sudden outburst startled her, and she stepped back. "Um, sure! Have you got it with you?"

Jim was becoming flustered. "No, no, I don't have it with me, no. But I could mail you something."

The woman smiled and tilted her head. "Sure, OK." She set the Barthelme book down on the shelf and started digging around in her purse. She came up with a scrap of paper and a pen. "I just love having strange men mail me things," she said, as she wrote her name and address on the scrap of paper. Then, "Here you go!" as she handed it to him.

Jim took it, and started backing away from her. "OK, thanks, um," his voice trailed off as he looked at the paper, "Thanks, Lisa! I'll put a story in the mail for you tonight."

Lisa chuckled and shook her head as she picked up the book. She looked at it for a moment, and then strode with it over to the cashier to buy it.

Jim skipped away through the empty shopping center, clutching the slip of paper as it if were the winning ticket in a million dollar lottery.

When he got home, he dug through his files, trying to decide what to send her. At last he settled on "The Empty City." He wrote a brief note, and attached it to the story. The note said, simply, "Hope you find this interesting." He signed it, and underneath his signature he wrote his phone number. Then he put the whole works into an envelope and took it to the mailbox. He was a happy man.

Chapter 77

"What time is it?" asked Umberto, as he and the Twins strode into the Saturn Cafe on a snowy Wednesday evening.

"Nine minutes till eight," said Peter.

"We're early," said Umberto.

They took their usual spots at their usual table and ordered their usual drinks. They set up their Icehouse pieces, ready to start a game as soon as Dave arrived. They even set Dave's pieces up for him, so that they could start as soon as he rolled in. Then they leaned back in their chairs, and awaited his arrival.

After a bit, Maria brought their drinks out to them, and they exchanged pleasantries.

"What time is it?" asked Umberto.

"Three minutes after eight," said Peter.

"He's late," said Umberto.

Peter shrugged. "He'll be along."

They sat drinking their beverages, waiting. They had nothing on their minds, so the conversation was sparse. The synthesist played a mellow, harmonious tune.

"What time is it?" asked Umberto.

"Nineteen minutes after eight," said Peter.

"He's late," said Umberto.

"Yep."

"He did say he'd be here, right?" asked Paul. "This day, this week, right?"

"That's what he said."

"Eight o'clock, right?"

"That's what he said."

Paul took out a small pocketknife and used it to dig the dirt out from under his fingernails.

Bert spent some time arranging the pieces on his stash pad in various different patterns.

Peter got up and disappeared in the direction of the restrooms.

"What time is it?" asked Umberto.

"Thirty three minutes after eight," said Peter.

"He's half an hour late," said Umberto.

Peter nodded.

Maria wandered by and asked if they wanted anything else. They asked for a plate of Tringos.

Paul suggested that they play a three player game while waiting for Dave, but the others didn't feel like it.

The synthesist played a piece consisting entirely of synthesized drums.

"What time is it?" asked Umberto.

"Quarter to nine," said Peter.

"He's late," said Umberto.

"Maybe something happened," said Paul. "Maybe he got stuck on a broken down subway, or maybe there was a track fire, or something."

"Maybe he just couldn't be bothered to meet up with us," said Umberto, bitterly. He ate the last of the Tringo crumbs, by licking his thumb and using its resulting stickiness to pick up the tiny bits of food.

"What time is it?" asked Umberto.

"Two minutes to nine," said Peter.

"He ain't coming," said Umberto.

Peter sighed. "I guess you're right, Bert. You want to play a three player game, or should we just get out of here?"

"I'm willing to play," said Paul.

Bert stood up. "I don't feel like it," he announced. "Let's just go."

"I think we should give him a little more time," said Paul. "He might still show up."

"I don't feel like waiting anymore," said Bert. "He ain't coming."

Then Peter stood up. "He's right, Paul. I think it's time we realized that Dave doesn't care about hanging around with us much anymore. He's more interested in his girlfriend than in us."

Paul stayed stubbornly in his chair. "Maybe he just lost track of time," he said, hopefully. "He's only an hour late."

"What do you mean, *only* an hour late! He's never an hour late! If he's this late, he ain't coming!"

"I still think we should wait a little longer," insisted Paul.

"You can wait if you want to," said Bert. "We're going."

"We might as well get on with our lives," said Peter. "Dave doesn't seem to have time for us anymore. I'm sure we'll see him now and then for a game, but we've just got to accept the fact that things aren't going to be the way they used to be."

Paul chewed on his tongue. Then he reluctantly stood up. "I guess you're right," he said, softly. "I guess you're right."

Outside, their feet crunched softly on newly fallen snow.

Chapter 78

Two days after Jim mailed a copy of "The Empty City" to Lisa, he got a phone call.

"Hello?" he said.

"Hello, Jim?" said a soft, female voice.

"Yes?"

"This is Lisa! You sent me this weird story!"

"Oh, yeah, Lisa!" said Jim, trying to sound as if he hadn't been waiting hopefully by the phone all day. "How's it going?"

"Oh, not too bad, not too bad," said Lisa.

"What'd you think of the story?"

"Well, it was kind of strange," she confided. "Now, I do like strange, so I did like it, but I got the impression that there was something going on in it that I didn't really understand."

"Hmm. Yes, well, I tried some symbolism there that I don't think really worked too well."

"But I still enjoyed."

"Good."

Silence. Jim decided it was now or never. He took the plunge.

"So listen, um, what are you doing tomorrow night? You want to get together? We could have dinner and talk about literature."

Jim listened to Lisa's breathing. He could hear her thinking about it, hesitating. The seconds dragged on. To Jim, it seemed like ten minutes elapsed before she spoke.

"OK," she said.

Jim's voice quavered with excitement as he asked for directions to her apartment, suggested a place and time, and worked out other details. He suggested they eat at "Trader Flip's," which was one of his favorite restaurants.

After they'd hung up, he jumped up and down and ran around his room, bursting with anticipation.

Chapter 79

Chemistry. That's what they call it when two people really hit it off, when their personalities fit together perfectly, each complementing the other, like cookies and milk or steak with a baked potato.

Chemistry. Lisa and Jim had it. It was clear from their first and only date.

They had dinner at an upscale Polynesian restaurant called Trader Flip's. It swept them away to a distant island in the South Pacific, where they were waited upon like a king and queen in an exotic, romantic setting.

Their table was in a secluded, darkened corner, with candles casting a flickering, magical glow over the table. Palm fronds hung from the ceiling, and a large Tiki statue regarded them unblinkingly from a nearby wall. Island music floated quietly across their eardrums.

The waiters spoke with thick accents, moving with slow, careful precision, asking not so much for their orders but for permission to bring them whatever exotic delights they desired. Jim and Lisa drank a powerful and exotic fruit drink from a volcano garnished with flowers. They nibbled at delicious appetizers served on a rotating round tray with a flaming brazier at its center. They were presented with hot towels, and then the main courses arrived. The waiters placed steaming plates of sumptuous foods before them, like offerings set before the Gods.

And during this whole magnificent meal, they talked. They discovered they had many common interests, that their ideas and opinions meshed together very well. They had chemistry. They felt comfortable in each other's company, they laughed at the same things, and they felt a similar attraction for each other.

After the meal they went back to her apartment. She lived alone in a small efficiency three blocks away from the Integer Avenue subway station.

Jim was very surprised by the appearance of the place. The room was barren, almost entirely empty. What she did possess seemed to be mostly packed up in cardboard boxes.

"Are you moving out or moving in?" asked Jim.

"Out," said Lisa. After locking the door behind her, she sat down on the mattress in the corner that served as her bed.

Her mood was different. A cloud had drifted across her mind.

"Where are you moving to?" asked Jim.

Lisa sighed. "If only," she said to herself.

Jim sat down next to her. "If only what?" he asked. His heart was pounding. What was wrong?

Lisa looked at Jim, her eyes drilling into his. They looked into each other's eyes for a long time. Then she looked down again.

"The timing is terrible," said Lisa. "I wish I'd met you a month ago, or that I'd never met you at all."

Jim worked hard to hold onto his composure, to keep from jumping up, from crying out, from screaming "What's going on?" As calmly as he could, he said "What's the matter?"

"I knew I shouldn't have called you," she said, shaking her head. "I knew it would just mess things up... but I didn't expect it to be like this."

Jim couldn't stand it anymore. He stood up and blurted out, "Will you please tell me what's going on?"

Lisa looked at the wall and said, "I joined the Peace Corps. I'm leaving tomorrow to live in Zambia."

Jim couldn't breathe, couldn't talk, couldn't think. He felt as if someone had clamped a monkey wrench onto his lung and was twisting it like a bolt.

Lisa stood up and put her arms around Jim. "I'm sorry," she said. "But I'm still glad I met you. I think you're really great. In some ways, I wish this hadn't happened, because it's torn a big hole in my logical thinking. But on the other hand, this evening was a magical night for me, and even if we never see each other again, I'm glad we've shared this much."

Jim was still too stunned to think, much less talk. Lisa led him over to her bed, and they sat down again. For a very long time, they just sat there, holding hands, thinking their own thoughts.

Later, they curled up together in Lisa's bed. Eventually, they went to sleep.

Chapter 80

In the morning, Jim felt OK. It was wonderful for him to wake and find someone warm and caring beside him, a sensation that he hadn't experienced in quite some time. It was bittersweet, since he knew it wouldn't happen again with this person; but even so, what they had shared had been magical indeed.

He lay awake for a long time without moving, Lisa's arm around him and her head resting on his chest. Finally, Lisa stirred, and they got up.

She had nothing in her refrigerator but some milk and margarine, and nothing in her pantry except some nearly stale bread, but their breakfast was still fine. They made toast in her oven, and washed it down with the milk.

After breakfast, they sat by the window, holding hands, watching the morning. They didn't talk. There was really nothing to say. It was like the last day of the world. They knew the world would end soon, and that they could do nothing to prevent it, and so they just sat, enjoying their remaining time together as much as they could.

At 9:30 that morning some movers arrived, and they took away all of Lisa's remaining boxes and furniture. She was left only with a small suitcase and a large purse.

At 11:15, she and Jim left the apartment. Lisa surrendered her key to the manager at the desk, and then she and Jim walked along Integer Avenue to the subway station. There, they parted.

She was to take a northbound train, which went out of the city and on to the Airport. He needed a southbound train. They stood silently on the platform, waiting to see whose train would arrive first. Inside, they each cried, but outside, they hid their emotions.

Then Lisa's train screeched into the station, and their goodbyes had to be brief. They kissed, and she got onto the train. "Goodbye!" she said.

"You have my address," said Jim, "So write to me, OK?"

"OK!" she said. Then the doors started to close, and they both called "Goodbye" again as the doors shut.

And Jim was left alone on the platform. He now felt no need to hide his emotions, and tears rolled down his face. He almost didn't notice when his train finally came.

Chapter 81

After a few days, Jim regained his composure. At first, he'd been so upset about losing Lisa so quickly after gaining her that he almost wished the whole thing had never happened. But bit by bit, he came to realize that he was very happy about it, that he had no regrets. Overall, the brief relationship had calmed him somewhat. It renewed his confidence. He realized that it was in fact possible for him to meet someone who cared about him and whom he could also care about. And this was important, as it was a fact he had often doubted in the months since Jennifer had turned him loose.

Though he still led a solitary life, he now had occasion to smile to himself, as if keeping a secret.

Chapter 82

At a few minutes before midnight, Jim wandered downstairs to the kitchen to make himself a snack. He couldn't find much food in the Asylum kitchen, and all he managed to scrounge up was some whole wheat toast and a mug of hot chocolate. Thus provisioned, he went back upstairs to his room to watch "The Twilight Zone." It was an excellent episode called "The After Hours," about the secret life of department store mannequins. After the Zone, he watched the first half of "Late Night with David Letterman," occasionally flipping channels to see parts of a rerun of "The Odd Couple."

At one o'clock in the morning, he snapped the set off and crawled into bed.

That night he had a dream.

He was at a railroad station. It was late at night, and the early winter air was cold and windy. He entered the station. Inside it was warm, but drafty, and the station, large and open, seemed very deserted. Three or four people sat waiting for the train, seated stiffly on the cold metal benches, their big, fully packed suitcases resting at their feet, their faces, blank and expressionless, still somehow displaying a sense of calm happiness.

Jim set down his own full suitcases and checked his pockets for perhaps the fiftieth time. Did his passport have the correct exit visas? Yes. Did he have enough cash to purchase a ticket? Yes. He checked the timetable. His train was due in ten minutes.

He approached the ticket window. The clerk was very old, and seemed very, very tired. Jim asked him for a one-way ticket. The clerk checked Jim's passport, then sold him the ticket. One hundred twenty two dollars and seventeen cents. The train was posted as being on time, due to arrive in seven minutes. Jim took his place on the benches with the others.

The time passed slowly, but at last Jim heard the shrill sound of the steam whistle as the train approached the station. Jim and the other passengers moved out onto the platform.

The train stopped and he stood waiting with the others as the arriving passengers disembarked. They moved very slowly. Their faces were also blank and expressionless, but there was no calm happiness in their eyes. They had a shell-shocked look, they seemed bewildered and confused, they wandered, aimlessly and listlessly, their eyes barely seeming to function. Some collapsed, helpless, on the platform. Guards appeared from somewhere, helping them to their feet, giving them directions as to where the rag-tag group should go.

Then they were boarding. As Jim awaited his turn, he again checked his passport, he again confirmed the existence of the ticket in his hand. Finally he was next. The conductor looked him over. He took Jim's ticket, and studied it. He took Jim's passport, and studied it even more closely. The conductor frowned. He stepped up into the train and conferred with another conductor. They talked in whispers, Jim could not hear their words. Finally the conductor faced Jim again. The train gave out a long, shrill whistle.

"I'm sorry," said the conductor.

"What?" squeaked Jim. His pulse raced, his breath was in quick, short bursts. "But I thought—"

"I'm sorry," said the conductor again. "Your ticket price will be refunded." The conductor swung up and into the passenger car and, with a lurch, the train began moving, very slowly at first but with gathering speed, vanishing into the distance.

The terrible cold silence of the winter night enveloped Jim, as he stood, amazed and confused, alone on the empty train platform. Then a guard appeared. "This way, sir," he said.

"Almost," thought Jim, as he went back into the Empty City.

Chapter 83

A cold winter rain sheeted down from a smooth gray sky. Dave bolted out of the Destiny Boulevard subway station and ran down the street through waves of heavy rain, becoming completely soaked by the time he got under the shelter of the entrance to his apartment building.

Inside, he shook himself off a bit, then headed for the mailboxes on his way toward the elevators. The mailbox contained a letter from Bert's brother in Los Angeles, two letters from charitable organizations wanting money, a mail order catalog from an adult videotape company, the phone bill, and a small package addressed to Dave.

The package was strange.

It was a small box, about the size of a paperback novel, though thicker. It was wrapped entirely in jet black paper. His name and address were written on the package in wite-out. It lacked a return address. The postmark, being black printing on a black surface, was unreadable, so he couldn't even tell where the package originated from.

Dave rode the elevator up to his apartment, pondering the black package. He couldn't even guess at who might have sent it to him. When he got inside the apartment, he tossed it onto a table in the hallway with the rest of the mail and went into his bedroom to change out of his freezing, wet clothing.

After this, Dave made himself some tea and examined the mail. He tore open the charity plea letters, looked them over, then threw them away. He opened the phone bill, studied it, and then attached it to the refrigerator with a magnet for his roommates to inspect. He flipped through the catalog. But he carefully avoided the package. Dave suddenly discovered, to his surprise, that he was afraid of it. After all, he didn't know what it was, or who had sent it to him, or even what city it had come from. It could be anything, a bomb, for example. Its strange black wrapping had an ominous feel to it.

Finally he overcame his fears and opened the package. Inside the black wrapping was a smooth high gloss black plastic box. Dave removed the lid. Inside was a note, written on black note paper in wite-out, and an object of some kind, wrapped in black cloth.

The note said:

DEAR SIR:

THE ENCLOSED ITEMS ARE ENTRUSTED TO YOU

PLEASE STORE THEM SAFELY.

WE WILL CONTACT YOU WHEN WE NEED THEM BACK.

WE MUST DEPEND ON YOU TO SAFEGUARD THEM.

IF ANYTHING HAPPENS TO THEM, YOU WILL COME TO REGRET IT.

WE RECOMMEND THAT YOU NOT TELL ANYONE ABOUT THIS.

A series of strange symbols graced the bottom of the note, resembling a signature of sorts.

Wrapped up in the cloth was a small cube, of some sort of heavy black metal, and also seven black metal tubes, like straws, only shorter, and also a thin disk of black plastic. Dave studied these items for a long while, but failed to reach any conclusion about them.

Then he became very annoyed. Who sent him this crap? Who did they think they were, that they could tell him to hold onto some junk of theirs and keep it safe until they were ready to take it back? Where did they get off with threatening him to keep this stuff for them without even telling him why, or for how long, or even who they were? Screw that, Dave thought. He took the weird items, rolled them up in the cloth, and shoved the whole thing back into the black plastic box. Then he went down the hall to the trash room and tossed it into the garbage chute. He heard it smash, 9 floors down.

He went back into the apartment and called the Martian Princess.

That evening they had dinner together and went to a movie, and Dave spent the night at her apartment. He completely forgot about the strange black package.

Chapter 84

At midnight, on a cold and gloomy Thursday night in late January, Jim sneezed. He had a bad cold, bordering on flu, and had therefore taken the day off of work. He had spent that day sitting around his room in the Asylum, feeling sick. He would lie on his couch and watch reruns on the rerun channel until he felt really sleepy, then he would crawl across the room to his bed and sleep for an hour or two. When he awoke he'd stagger downstairs for some OJ, then return to the couch and the television.

By now, he was feeling a little bit better.

He lay there on the couch with the flickering glow of the television washing over him, changing the channels with the remote control when things got dull.

"Just sit right back and you'll hear a tale, a tale of a fateful"
- Click -
"These are the voyages of the Starship Enterprise, her"
- Click -
"This one's definitely softer"
- Click -
"Ladies and gentlemen, he's young, he's personable, Mr. Paul Shaffer"
- Click -
"a journey into a wondrous land, whose boundaries are that of imagi-"
- Click -
"Belly gunner to bombardier"
- Click -
"Nice shootin', Tex"
- Click -
"Colonel Hogan, you are not fooling me one bit"
- Click -
"Well, how do we know it's not a fake, it looks like a fake to me"
- Click -
"the Professor and Mary Ann, here on Gilligan's Isle!"

Jim left it on channel 10 and crawled downstairs to the kitchen for some more orange juice.

When he returned, Gilligan was running down the path toward the lagoon. "Hey, Perfesser, Skipper, Skipper, Perfesser!" shouted Gilligan as he ran.

"Not now, Gilligan, can't you see the Professor and I are busy?"

"Yeah, but Skipper," protested Gilligan.

And at that moment, Gilligan tripped. He stumbled, and Jim saw his shoulder impact with the inside of the glass of his picture tube. The television teetered on its stand, then toppled off and hit the floor.

There was a loud flash of light, and the stench of burning electronics filled the air. And Jim looked, and Gilligan, the Skipper, and the Professor were all standing in his room, live and in person.

"Now look what you've done, Gilligan!" bellowed the Skipper. "You've broken the Television Barrier!"

"Gee, I'm real sorry, Skipper," said Gilligan. "Here, I'll fix it." Gilligan picked up the television and tried to put it back on the stand. In doing so, he stumbled backwards and stepped on the Skipper's big toe.

"Yow!" shouted the Skipper. "Look, Gilligan, just drop that thing! The Professor and I will take care of it!"

"Just drop it?" asked Gilligan.

"Yes!" shouted the Skipper.

"OK!" said Gilligan, and dropped the television on the Skipper's foot. The Skipper bellowed again, even more loudly, and then took off his cap and struck Gilligan on the head with it.

Jim regarded these characters and his broken TV with some dismay from the doorway.

"Hey, Skipper," asked Gilligan, "Who's that guy?"

"It's probably the owner of the television set you just ruined," said the Skipper. "Now shut up."

The Skipper took off his Skipper's hat and crushed it to his chest. Taking a few tentative steps towards Jim, he politely said "Uh, excuse us?"

Jim looked around and said "You mean me?" I must really be sick, Jim thought. Lynda shouted up at Jim from her room, which was right below his. "What's all the noise up there?" Her voice was barely audible.

The Professor meanwhile had put the television back on its stand and was studying it intently. "Skipper," he said, "do you realize what this means?"

"That we're gonna be rescued?" suggested the Skipper.

"No!" said the Professor, "Much worse than that! With the Television Barrier broken, it means we're all free to enter the Real World!"

"Oh, boy!" said Gilligan.

"You don't understand," said the Professor. "Gilligan, can you imagine what would happen if strange fictional characters like ourselves were allowed to roam about in the Real World? And I have no reason to believe that the hole in the barrier is limited to our show alone. Why, any minute now, all manner of strange beings could come out of that TV and into the Real World! There'll be gunslingers from old westerns attacking giant monsters from cheesy science fiction shows, late night talk show hosts interviewing famous historical personalities, and housewives from 50s sitcoms trying to tidy up after World War II bombing missions!"

"Wow!" said Gilligan, "That sounds great!"

"No!" said the Professor, "It would be terrible! It could spell the end of the world! We've got to stop it!"

"Well, gee, Professor, what can we do?" asked the Skipper.

"The first thing we've got to do is to somehow keep everyone else in Television Land out of the Real World."

Gilligan picked up Jim's remote control unit.

"Hey, Perfesser, maybe this thing can help!"

Unwittingly, Gilligan pressed the button that changed the channel. Jim heard the sound of "Star Trek" transporters engaging.

Captain Kirk, Mr. Spock, and Dr. McCoy appeared in his room.

"Phasers on stun," said Captain Kirk.

"Oops!" said Gilligan, laughing, "Wrong button! I'll try a different one."

"No!" shouted the Skipper. "Here, give me that!"

"No, Skipper, I can figure it out!"

In the ensuing struggle, the channel switcher got pressed many times. With each press, as the Skipper tried to wrestle the remote out of Gilligan's hands, more Television personalities appeared in Jim's room. David Letterman, along with the lovely and talented Teri Garr. Cary Grant. The Poppin' Fresh Dough Boy and two small children, eager consumers of Pillsbury Coffee Cake. The crew of a B-17 Bomber. Sergeant Schultz and Colonel Klink. Mary Ann, Ginger, and Mr. and Mrs. Howell. Rod Serling. Mr. Whipple. Major Anthony Nelson, his buddy Major Healy, and Jeannie. And many others.

At last, the Skipper wrenched the remote control unit from Gilligan's hands. "Sorry, Skipper," apologized Gilligan.

"Fascinating," said Mr. Spock.

"You have just entered The Twilight Zone," intoned Rod Serling.

The noise grew louder and louder as the people jammed into Jim's room questioned their predicament. By now, Lynda had come upstairs to investigate, and she was pounding on Jim's door and yelling at him to turn down the volume on his TV set. Jim's headache throbbed as the noise grew more and more intense, until he felt like someone had rammed a fork into his scalp and was pushing it in deeper with every heartbeat, until he was sure the blood vessels in his forehead were on the point of bursting.

"BE QUIET!" he bellowed, as he pushed his way through the crowd. Jim went over to the wall socket and yanked out the television plug. Instantly, the room became silent, and everyone in it vanished. For a brief moment, dozens of tiny points of light floated in the room, each located at the spot where, a moment before, a television personality had been standing. Then, slowly, these points of light also faded, and Jim was alone.

Lynda opened the door to Jim's room. "What on Earth is going on in here?" she demanded.

"Something went kinda screwy with my TV set," said Jim. "I finally had to unplug it. Sorry."

Lynda raised her eyebrows, shook her head, and went back downstairs.

Jim staggered over to his bed, collapsed on it, and fell asleep.

Chapter 85

In the morning, Dave remembered the strange black package, with a bit of fear and regret. Throwing it away was probably not the smartest thing in the world. But as he thought about it further, he stood his ground. He was not about to be pushed around by people he didn't even know. They were wrong if they thought they could force him to take orders from them.

Over breakfast, he told the Princess about it. She seemed amused by the package, and thought Dave had made a big mistake in throwing it away. They argued for a long time about it. Dave insisted that whoever had sent it to him had been way out of line in expecting him to be their custodian, and that his action had been perfectly reasonable. However, as that day wore on he became increasingly concerned about what would happen if whoever sent him the stuff suddenly demanded it back.

Chapter 86

In the morning, Jim considered his problem. He couldn't quite convince himself that what had happened the night before was simply a fever induced dream, and he was afraid that plugging the TV set back in would just re-open the door through the barrier. This was a situation that Jim didn't wish to encounter again. So he wrapped the cord around the set, took it down the street to a neighborhood dumpster, and heaved it in. It smashed satisfyingly.

Later that day, he went out to the Value Village Thrift Store and bought an old black and white TV set that seemed to work OK.

Chapter 87

Peter decided it was time to empty the trash. The can was overflowing, and the associated stench was becoming overpowering. So he pulled the corners of the bag together, extracted it (with some difficulty) from the trash can, and wrapped a twist tie around the top. Then he hauled it out of the apartment and down the hall to the trashroom.

Each floor had its own trashroom, located just outside the elevators, where the residents of the floor deposited their trash. Each trashroom had a trash chute, at the bottom of which was a huge dumpster. Trash that was too big or too volatile to be dropped down the chute was simply deposited on the floor of the trashroom.

Peter opened the door to the tenth floor trashroom and was astonished by what he saw.

A mannequin!

With a quick glance down the halls to make sure that no one would see him, Peter grabbed the mannequin and hauled it back to the apartment. He had no idea what he would do with it, but it was too good to let get thrown away in the trash.

Paul looked up at him, greatly surprised, as he dragged the mannequin in.

"Where'd you get that?" he asked.

Peter leaned the mannequin against the wall, shut the door, and quickly tried to catch his breath. "It was in the trashroom," he said, "Someone was throwing it out."

Paul stood up and looked at it, appraisingly. "Hmm, not bad," he concluded. "Her left arm is kind of messed up, and there's this hole in her leg, but otherwise, she's in pretty good shape. What do you want to do with her?"

"I don't know," said Peter. "I just grabbed it. It was too good to ignore. I figured we'd think of something to do with it."

Bert had by this time heard the commotion and had wandered out to see what was up. "Wow," he said, "Where'd you get it?"

"In the trashroom," said Peter, growing tired of repeating himself. "It was being thrown out."

"The question before us now," said Paul, "is what to do with it. Any ideas?"

Bert said "We could dress it up like Dave, and then we'd have a fourth for Icehouse!"

It wasn't very funny, and the others didn't really laugh. But Bert wasn't deterred. "Or," he went on, "we could make it look like Doug, and leave it in the elevator to bug people."

"That might not be bad," said Paul. "Or maybe we could do something similar, like maybe bringing it onto the subway and setting it up in a chair to look like a normal person, to see how long it takes for someone to realize it's a dummy."

Peter was studying the thing. "I wonder if..." he mumbled. Then, with a sweeping motion, he yanked the mannequin's arm off. "Yes! We can take it apart!"

Paul wasn't impressed. "So, what good is that?"

"Well, I don't know. It seems like it might be useful, that's all."

After standing around looking at it for a while, they sat down. They discussed various ideas, but couldn't come up with anything that really interested them. They thought about dropping it off of the roof, but decided against this since it would destroy the mannequin. They thought about putting it outside of someone's window, peering in, but decided it wouldn't be scary enough. They even thought about taking

THE EMPTY CITY

it to the graveyard and burying it up to its waist, rigging it to look like a corpse rising from the dead. But they figured it might sit out there for days, unnoticed, and that it might get damaged by the elements.

Ultimately, they just dressed it in normal clothes and stood it up in Dave's room, hoping it would scare him out of his wits when he came home.

Chapter 88

At a few minutes before one o'clock in the morning, Dave quietly unlocked the door to apartment 1017 and went in. The others were asleep, and the apartment was dark.

He was in a bitter mood. That evening he had taken the Princess to see a movie called "Neon Highways." Afterwards, they'd had a big argument. He had hated the movie, and she had loved it. During the entire subway ride home, Dave had run down parts of the movie that he thought were stupid, but the Princess refused to acknowledge his arguments. She had enjoyed the film, and that was that. After listening to him for awhile, it seemed to Dave that she'd started to ignore him, to tune him out. And finally, when they'd gotten back to her apartment, she'd asked him not to stay, making some excuse about having to get up early in the morning. And so, with great frustration, Dave had walked back out to the Zephyr Heights subway station and taken a train back home.

He flipped on the light to his room and saw a mannequin wearing some of his clothes. He wasn't amused. He crawled into bed and went to sleep.

Chapter 89

The harsh winter cold bit at Jim's earlobes as he walked through the streets of the City. However, it was warm and pleasant inside the Saturn Cafe.

Once Jim was admitted, he went straight to the back table where The Four always preferred to sit. Although they hadn't been frequenting the Cafe as much as they used to, they'd all managed to get together tonight for a few games of Icehouse.

Jim greeted them, then went around behind their table and leaned against the carpeted wall, to watch them play. This game was well underway; Umberto had already used up all of his small pyramids.

A waitress approached and Jim ordered a beaker of C-tea. Neon light gleamed off of her halo-like headpiece as she walked away.

Peter and Paul each played several of their small pyramids, followed by a brief flurry of activity by Dave and Bert.

Jim watched the game with detached interest. His mind was on other things. He listened to the music of the synthesist and pondered the plot of a short story he was trying to write.

In the Pit, the synthesist created musical sounds that swam through the room and drifted up to the ceiling. He was attempting to create musical images. He would form an image in his mind, then create music to represent it. He thought of misty dew drops, dripping from tropical leaves in the rain forest, then played random, staccato, flute-like tones on his keyboard. He thought of horseshoe crabs, crawling across a hot, sandy beach, and played a slow, deep-throated melody, ambling along under the rainy dew drops. He thought of nebulas, gradually shifting over the eons from purple to red to yellow, changing slowly before a backdrop of a million stars in the dark, black sky, and played a shimmering, acoustical harmony, rolling along to the slow beat of the crabs, as they crawled across the beach.

Jim became dimly aware that someone was standing near him, off to the right. He looked, and found it was true. She was an attractive looking woman, wearing a black dress and a white scarf. As Jim turned his head to look at her, she turned her head away, looking instead at the Icehouse table.

Jim returned his gaze to the Icehouse game in progress, but before long, he could tell from his peripheral vision that she was looking at him again. He looked back, and she looked away. They repeated this sequence several times. Each time he looked at her, she looked away. When he again looked away, she turned back to look at him.

Then they both looked at each other at the same time.

"Are you looking at me?" Jim suddenly asked.

"No!" said the woman, and laughed. They both looked back at the Icehouse table.

"Who do you think will win?" asked Jim.

After a short pause, the woman said "The fat guy."

Jim snickered. "Bert? Not this time. Dave's got it sewn up."

Synthesizer tones cascaded over the crowd in the Cafe. Waves crashed against the beach. The horseshoe crabs continued their lumbering crawl. Dave came out the winner, though he only iced his opponents by a narrow margin. "That wasn't such a great game," Jim said to the woman. "Usually these guys make them more interesting." He took a sip of his C-tea, then looked back at her. "Care for a game?" he said.

"I don't have a set," she said.

"Neither do I," said Jim, "We'll use a house copy."

Jim led the woman over to an empty table, and they sat down. He slid open a concealed drawer under the table top and began removing his Icehouse pieces. Then the woman understood, and located her own drawer. "Actually, I'm a terrible player," she confided.

"So am I," said Jim. "It takes years of practice to get good."

They began to play. The woman was indeed quite unskilled, and Jim relaxed his own stance a bit in order to even things up. He still won easily, and by the end of the game she was laughing at her mistakes.

The waitress stopped by, asking if Jim wanted a refill. He agreed, and asked the woman if she too wanted a drink. She declined.

A tall man in a dark green suit entered the Cafe. He stood in the doorway with a disoriented expression on his face, as if looking for someone. Then his expression changed, and he walked briskly towards Jim and the woman. As he drew near, the woman turned, and seeing him, smiled broadly.

"Sorry I'm late," he said, kissing the woman on the cheek.

"It's OK," she said, standing up. "Bye," she said to Jim, "It was nice meeting you."

"Bye," said Jim, vacantly, as he watched the couple stroll away.

"Who was that?" Jim heard the man ask.

"Oh, just this guy I met while waiting for you." The woman's voice faded away into the background noise of the Cafe. The horseshoe crabs were gone. Instead, seagulls now drifted on the gentle ocean breeze. Jim sipped his C-tea until it was gone, then went out into the night.

The harsh winter cold bit at Jim's earlobes as he walked through the streets of the City.

Chapter 90

Peter and Paul were sitting in the kitchen of the Asylum, leaning back on the chairs with their feet up on the table. They had nothing much to do, and didn't feel like hanging around with Bert, since Dave now joined them so rarely, and so they were spending their Sunday afternoon languishing at the Asylum.

Pauline wandered downstairs to get a glass of ice water. She nodded at the Twins, but said nothing.

"Hey, Pauline," said Peter, "If you had a mannequin, what would you do with it?"

Peter had not expected much of a reaction to his casual question, and was amazed at her response. She whirled around at him, eyes wide with excitement. "Why, have you got one?"

Peter squirmed, and admitted that they did.

Pauline shut the refrigerator door and shouted "Wow! Where'd you get it! HOW did you get it? I've always wanted a mannequin! How much you want for it? I'll buy it from you!"

Peter forced her back to the original question. "Why do you want one? What would you do with it?"

Pauline sat down at the table. "I have a couple of ideas. What kind of mannequin is it? Male? Female?"

"Female."

"Complete body or just the torso?"

"Complete body."

Pauline jumped up again, squealing with excitement. "Oooh! It's perfect! At least loan it to me!"

Peter was becoming impatient to know what Pauline had in mind. "Look, you can *have* the dang thing if you just let us in on what you'd do with it."

Pauline freaked out. "Really! WOW! OK, you can help with everything! How soon can you get it over here?"

Chapter 91

The subway rumbled through the tunnel, lights flashing past the window in blurred streaks. Jim sat on the plastic bench, shoulders slumped, his chin on his chest, looking down but not really looking, his mind lethargic and empty. His only thoughts were of home and how good it would be to get there.

Several chairs away, he could see a young couple. They were arguing about something, in hushed voices, wanting to shout at each other, but not wanting to draw attention to themselves by shouting. They spoke in whispered shouts. Jim couldn't really make out much of what they were saying, he could only understand occasional phrases.

"You still didn't have to say that to him"

It reminded Jim of times when, as a kid, he would lie awake in bed listening to his parents talking in their room, across the hall from his.

"I just don't see what difference it makes"

Jim would be lying in his bed, with the lights in his room turned off, but at his insistence, the door left open and the hallway light left on. And since the door was open, he could hear bits of his parents' conversation as the words drifted across the hall and into his room.

"You should have at least apologized"

He would lie there, straining to figure out exactly what they were saying, or even what they were talking about. Sometimes Jim could hear them quite clearly, but at other times the voices in the darkness were distant and indistinct, and his mind would wander away to other topics, like monsters and cookies.

"I just don't see what there was to apologize for"

And Jim could always tell when they were talking about him.

Sometimes he even thought he woke up when their topic of conversation shifted to him.

"You're crazy"

At the next subway stop, the young couple disembarked, taking their hushed argument with them.

Chapter 92

Jim got home from work at twenty minutes after six. He entered the Asylum, tired and glad to be home.

He started towards the stairs, planning to go straight up to his room, but he heard some strange noises coming from the kitchen and went that way instead, in order to investigate.

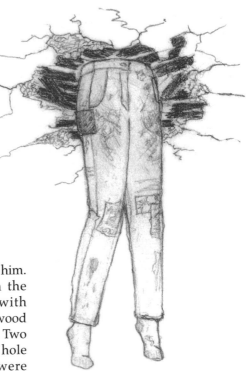

What he saw amazed him. A hole had appeared in the ceiling of the kitchen, with plaster and broken bits of wood scattered all over the floor. Two legs protruded from the hole above him. The legs were wearing a pair of patched old jeans, which Jim recognized as belonging to Pauline.

"Pauline?" he said, "Are you OK?"

He heard Pauline's voice shouting in the room above him. "Jim? Oh, thank God! Help me! The floor collapsed under me! I'm stuck!"

Jim felt a rush of adrenaline as he ran up the stairs to rescue his housemate. His mind was crowded with confused thoughts. Are all the floors in this house that weak? If she's really stuck, how can I get her out? How long has she been like this? Where's everyone else?

Pauline's room was located directly over the kitchen, and Jim burst in without knocking. Pauline's upper half was sticking up from a hole in the floor near the back of her room. She was facing away from Jim.

On hearing the noise of his entrance, she said "Boy, am I glad you're here, Jim. I've been stuck like this for an hour."

Jim, nearing panic, knelt down at Pauline's side. "What can I do? Are you hurt? Can you move at all?"

Then he looked at Pauline's face, and nearly died of astonishment and embarrassment. It wasn't her at all. It was a mannequin.

Pauline burst out laughing and emerged from her hiding place behind the bed. Peter and Paul also popped out, laughing, from their spots behind piles of bulky clutter.

"We got you!" they howled.

What they had done, of course, was to bolt the lower half of the mannequin to the ceiling in the kitchen, and the upper half to the floor in Pauline's room. Then Pauline had realistically painted the ceiling and floor around the edges of the mannequin, so that both looked like they had gaping holes. Lastly, they'd scattered broken plaster, dust, and dirt onto the floor, and had dressed the two parts of the mannequin in Pauline's clothes.

Jim had fallen right into the trap. Pauline and the twins screamed with laughter.

Later that evening, they repeated the practical joke, with varying degrees of success, on Lynda, Suzanne, and Wanda, and also Torrence and Maria.

Chapter 93

The show opened on a Saturday in early March. The opening was well attended, but was not as jammed as the Emperor and the other organizers had hoped. A large percentage of those attending were, as it turned out, Martians.

"Visions of the Martian Civilization" was shown at the Teldman Gallery, on the east side of the city, a block from the Randall Square station, on the purple line. Tall thin banners were hung on either side of the main entrance, proclaiming the show to the world. The title of the show ran diagonally along the side of the banners. The banner on the left was black and showed Mars floating in space; the right hand banner was red and depicted a stylized Martian cityscape, of spheres and pyramids.

The Teldman was a fine old gallery, with polished wood floors and high lofty ceilings. The sounds of the visitors' quiet discussions echoed through the halls, mixed with the clicking of hard-soled shoes on hardwood floors.

The program described the concept of the show.

All of the works presented in this show were done by artists from a group called The Children of Mars. This group of artists is united by one common factor: they all have red hair. The group believes that they are descendents of the ancient inhabitants of the Red Planet of Mars, who, unlike Earthlings, had red hair. The works in this show are thought to be recreations of elements of the ancient civilization on Mars, now long dead, revived through race memories buried in the artists' subconscious.

Some parts of the show are organized according to what the artists believed was the use and function of their recreations. Other exhibits are not organized at all, simply because the original purpose of the items on display is not understood. Here, interpretation of the artifacts on display is left up to the imagination of the visitor.

The show occupied five rooms, four small rooms around a larger central chamber. The center room was the show's most impressive; it was a collaborative effort in which many of the Martian artists had participated, and it depicted a complete Martian city. As you stood in the center of the room, you saw ancient stone buildings, pyramids, spheres, and obelisks. The red surface of Mars stretched away from the city in all directions. A canal sliced out from the city to the north. The closest four structures, two spheres and two pyramids, were physically present, having been carved from huge blocks of stone. The structures further away, as well as the Martian desert, the horizon, and the sky above, were depicted in a vast and highly detailed trompe l'oeil painting. The door into the room opened through one of the buildings, a large pyramid, which gave the visitor the effect of stepping out of a building and into the open air of Mars.

The illusion was maintained down to the smallest detail. Fine red sand covered the floor of the exhibit. The room was under careful climate control, being kept darker and cooler than the other rooms of the museum. Additionally, actors formed part of the exhibit. A number of red haired people were paid to stay in the room full time and behave as real Martians might have behaved. In one corner, several Martians sat at a round stone table playing Icehouse, using a set made from naturally colored stone crystals. In another corner, one or two Martians sat busying themselves with various Martian "artifacts," acting as if they not only understood their functions but were actually utilizing them. The actors treated the visitors to the exhibit as if they were simply other Martians, wandering by a busy street corner in a city on Mars.

The outer exhibit halls were more traditional. The walls were hung with paintings, and sculptures squatted on pedestals and looked out from under glass cases. Some of the paintings presented realistic views of Martian life, others were far more abstract and non-representational, colorful arrangements of geometric shapes and so forth. The sculptures all tended to be bizarre objects which the artist clearly hoped would seem like normal items from Martian life. These included painted metal rods, spheres with holes at random points, cubic boxes containing odd substances, and pyramids inscribed with weird symbols.

In one room, under a large sign that said "Feel free to touch," was a table laid out with a number of interactive sculptures. The most popular of these was a Marxhausen Stardust, but others attracted some attention as well. A small heptahedron, made of purple metal, breathed out a fragrant mist. A black plastic rod felt strangely warm to the touch, while a similar white rod was distinctly cold. Other sculptures did nothing but were still pleasing to touch and hold, such as a small three sided pyramid, covered with strange raised symbols, and a glass sphere containing thousands of tiny gold metal beads.

Pauline's sculpture, "Martian Toaster," was on display in a glass case with a large pile of "Martian Money," this being small gold coins of various triangular shapes. On the wall behind this, a series of pen and ink drawings by the Martian Princess was on view. Also in this room were three Icehouse sets, and an explanation of the game and its origin.

The overall tone of the exhibit was one of historical mustiness rather than Avant Garde art. The Children of Mars wanted the exhibit to seem archaeological rather than creative, as if the objects on display were not mere works of art but were instead items actually recovered from the ruined cities on Mars and brought back to be displayed, like relics from the Mayans or from Ancient Egypt.

The gift shop sold souvenirs of the show, including T-shirts, reproductions of some of the sculptures, postcards of some of the paintings, deluxe Icehouse sets, and cloth bags filled with Martian coins.

Art critics gave the show mixed reviews. Most seemed to like the art very much, but felt that the artists took themselves too seriously.

Chapter 94

Jim bought a camera.

It was not his first camera, but it was his first good camera. He had a little pocket instamatic camera, the simple little box with no controls other than the button you pressed to take the picture. It took OK snapshots.

But one day Jim decided to get a real camera, with real control mechanisms, such as an adjustable focus. So he bought a completely manual camera, a big black 35mm machine. It had a huge lens, which, he was surprised to discover, was purchased separately from the camera body, and a big flash gun, also purchased separately. He acquired all of this, plus film and batteries, with money he'd been saving for no real purpose, and though it blew his entire bankroll, he was excited and pleased with his new equipment.

He took it all home and started playing. The camera seemed enormous when compared to the little thing he used to stuff into his hip pocket, and it also seemed terribly fragile... but he figured he'd adjust to it soon enough.

He didn't put film into it right away, but instead walked around the Asylum, focusing on things, taking pretend pictures. He felt he had a lot of learning to do, learning how to focus, how to set the f-stop to allow the right amount of light in, how to get the film loaded, how to set the flash up properly, and so on. But he played around with it for awhile and learned the basics quickly enough.

Then he loaded it up with film, and shot the entire roll, again walking around the Asylum, shooting pictures of things. He took photos of different rooms, with different amounts of light and different settings of the camera. He went outside and took some daylight shots of the outside of the Asylum, and of the street.

When he'd finished off the roll, he went out to the local one hour photo developing shop and had the photos developed. On the whole, they looked good, and Jim was happy with his accomplishments.

When he got home, he loaded up another roll and convinced some of his housemates to let him take their pictures. He photographed Pauline working on a sculpture and Lynda playing her sax, but neither of them was happy about the photo opportunities and they only put up with a few shots each. Wanda on the other hand said she'd be willing to pose for as many photos as Jim wanted to take as long as she got prints of them, and Jim soon figured out why. She insisted on changing into a different one of her tie-dyed shirts every few minutes. She obviously wanted the photos to record the shirts she made, but that was fine with Jim.

Soon Jim was back at the one hour developers, and again he was pleased with his results.

And so, over the days and weeks that followed, Jim took a lot of pictures and gradually developed some skill with his new camera.

Chapter 95

Jim placed an ad in the 'Wanted' section of the City Paper classifieds which read as follows:

Amateur photographer seeks attractive woman with very long hair (waist length or longer) for photo studies. Payment in prints.

The ad also listed his name and phone number.

Jim had two goals in mind when he placed the ad. First, he was interested in shooting pictures of long haired women, because he wanted to practice taking pictures, and he considered models with long hair to be a bit more challenging to photograph than short haired women. He hoped to build up a portfolio. Secondly, he really liked long hair. He thought it looked great and also felt that he got along better with women with longer hair. It seemed to him that women with short hair were driven too much by the laws of fashion, while women who let their hair grow long were more real and less made up. So by placing the ad, Jim figured he might, just might, meet someone he could really get along with.

Three women called. The first was oriental, and had beautiful black hair, very straight and long. The second had brown hair, kind of frizzy and not quite waist length. The third, whose name was Lori, had incredible hair, a wonderful, rich blond, straight and smooth, very thick and very long, reaching down almost to her knees. Jim set up times to meet them and shot a roll of film on each. His pictures concentrated entirely on their hair; he shot pictures of their hair hanging down their backs, of them brushing their hair, of them lying on the floor with their hair brushed out in all directions, and this sort of thing.

Jim didn't seem to hit it off at all with either of the first two. With Lori, however, he appeared to have at least some slim chance, since she didn't appear to be dating anyone else and since she and Jim had gotten along well during the photo session. So, unlike with the first two, when Jim dropped off the photos from their first session, he asked if she'd be willing to pose for him again. She seemed delighted with the pictures and agreed.

So Jim met her again and shot another roll of photos. When he dropped these off, he suggested a third session... and decided to press his luck. He asked Lori if she'd be willing to pose a bit more, uh, "dramatically," than she had before. Jim had in mind a series of "Godiva" pictures, photos in which the model would be nude or semi-nude, but would be clothed, as it were, with her hair. Jim tried to make it very clear that the photos would not show any actual nudity. To his surprise and great delight, she agreed. They settled on the following Saturday, at her apartment.

At the appointed hour, Jim arrived. Lori introduced Jim to her two roommates, a couple of giggly, slightly overweight sisters, who promptly disappeared, as if on cue, to go shopping.

The apartment was very nice, a bit underfurnished perhaps, but roomy and clean. The living room had a wide, barren, light blue wall, which was a perfect neutral background to shoot against, and Jim quickly commented on this. Jim and Lori chatted awkwardly for a minute or two. She offered him a drink, and he accepted a Coke. They both tried hard to act casual and relaxed, but the tension was very thick. They both felt strange about what they were planning to do, and, while it was never discussed, the subject nevertheless loomed over them. Finally Jim said, "Well, I suppose we should get started." She nodded.

He began to busy himself with his camera equipment, and she disappeared down the hallway and into one of the bedrooms. After about a minute, she emerged again. She walked towards Jim very slowly. The dingy jeans and white T-shirt she'd been wearing before were gone. Her hair hung down in even masses on both sides of her head, neatly covering her breasts. She also had some of her hair draped over her left arm, which she held against her stomach so that the hair fell straight down, concealing her lower abdomen just so.

Jim tingled with excitement and delight. He smiled broadly at Lori and told her she looked fantastic, in fact perfect. Then he stopped talking and took some pictures. Lori walked past him to the plain living room wall to pose for a few more. Jim noticed as she turned her back to him that she had actually separated her hair into three clumps: two for either side up front, and a third which hung straight down her back, concealing her backside.

Jim shot an entire roll of film and immediately wished he'd brought another. With each shot, he worried about the flash settings, and halfway through he switched to available light photography so that if he was screwing up the flash shots the effort wouldn't be a total waste.

Each time he asked her to change to a new pose, Lori would comply very slowly. It was fascinating to watch her move. She had such grace, yet each movement she made was very slow and deliberate, calculated and exact. She was always very careful to make sure that her hair covered her where it mattered, not moving a muscle unless protected by this special shield. Jim found it fascinating and delightful, and while his male instincts hoped she would at some point goof it up, that she'd let the hair slip and permit him a glimpse of what was being kept hidden, he still had to admire her control and precision.

Finally Jim announced that he was out of film. Lori smiled, and then retreated to the room in the back, again walking with very slow and stately grace, her hair always remaining strategically placed. When the door shut behind her, Jim packed up his camera.

ANDREW LOONEY

After a few minutes, she emerged, dressed again in the jeans and T-shirt, with her hair bound at the back in a pony tail. She and Jim both felt a rush of relief, and, for the first time, were able to talk and laugh and be relaxed in each other's company. Before long, fearing to outstay his welcome, Jim made for the door, promising to deliver a set of prints as soon as he got the film developed.

He stood in the hallway, with Lori looking out at him through the open door. "Thanks," he said, and turned to go. Then he turned back, and said, "Um, are you doing anything tonight?"

She slowly shook her head, no.

"How's about dinner?" asked Jim, trembling.

She nodded, with slow, careful grace.

Jim grinned a toothy grin and said "Great, I'll pick you up at 7:00, OK?"

She nodded again, and slowly shut the door, never taking her eyes off of Jim.

Jim went home feeling immensely happy, stopping on the way back to drop off the film at the developers.

Chapter 96

At eleven minutes before eight o'clock, Jim and Lori approached the Saturn Cafe. Jim was wearing a white shirt and white slacks, and Lori was wearing a black dress. She had her hair tied back in a single, long braid.

They stopped, and stood before the door. Lori looked at the small icon of Saturn, then at Jim. Jim said nothing, but merely gazed at the door with a blank expression on his face.

"What is this?" asked Lori.

Jim seemed to return slowly to consciousness. "Oh," he said, "This is the Saturn Cafe. It's very exclusive. The management is deciding whether or not to let us in."

Before Lori had a chance to reply, the door clicked. "Ah," said Jim, "in we go."

The Cafe was crowded. The synthesizer music pulsed heavily under the noise of the people. Jim steered Lori towards a small table in the corner. A waitress moved through the pools of light and arrived at their table. "What can I get you?"

"I'll have the Chicken Kiev and a C-tea," said Jim.

"OK," said the waitress. She noted his order and then looked expectantly at Lori.

"Oh," said Lori, "I don't know. Um, I guess I'll have a salad."

The waitress floated away. "This place is amazing," said Lori, with a dazed tone in her voice.

"Pretty cool, huh?" Jim reclined in his chair.

"Yeah," said Lori, sitting up and looking around in every direction. "The lights, and the music... and the people!"

Jim simply smiled. The waitress brought him his C-tea, and he sipped at it slowly.

"What are they playing over there?" asked Lori, pointing to a group playing Icehouse.

"That's Icehouse," replied Jim.

"Oh, yeah? I've always meant to learn that," said Lori.

"I can teach you right now, if you want," said Jim.

"Really? That'd be great!"

Jim was already removing a stash of pyramids from the table's concealed drawer. He set up a couple of simple examples, and began explaining the rules of the game to Lori. But he had never tried to teach someone to play Icehouse before, and soon found himself running into trouble. He rambled as he tried to remember all the rules. By the time he got to Over-icing and Attack Restructuring, he could see that Lori's eyes were glazing over.

"Actually, " said Jim, "the original game of Icehouse isn't really the best one to start with. It's pretty complicated. How's about I show you a different game for Icehouse pieces? There are actually quite a few good ones. I know one called IceTowers which is kind of similar to Icehouse, but a lot easier to learn. Wanna try that?"

Lori nodded enthusiastically. "Yes, please!"

"OK, then" said Jim. "For this game, you'll need one of these hollow sets, since we'll be stacking the pyramids up, like this." Jim quickly went through the basics of Stacking, Mining, and Splitting, and this time, Lori didn't find his explanations bewildering. In fact, they were already playing their first game when the waitress arrived with their food.

"We'll have to try this again later," said Jim, pushing the pieces aside.

"Deal!" said Lori, picking up her fork with a smile.

Later on, after eating, Jim again scattered the Icehouse pieces out onto the table. He and Lori played a couple of quick games of IceTowers, then they left the Saturn Cafe, heading for the Asylum.

Once there, Jim introduced his new friend to some of his housemates. Lynda told Lori a little about Bill's adventures, and when Pauline told Lori the story of her "fall" through the floor, Jim's face went red with embarrassment.

"Nice girl!" Torrence said to Jim, as they stood in the kitchen waiting for Lynda, Pauline and Lori to stop giggling amongst themselves. "Great hair, too!"

"Isn't she amazing?" said Jim with a grin.

Chapter 97

At eleven minutes before ten o'clock, Dave and the Martian Princess approached the Saturn Cafe. Dave was wearing a black trenchcoat and the Princess wore her red camo jacket.

They stopped, and stood before the door. They gazed at the small icon of Saturn, and presently they heard the familiar click of the door being unlocked.

The Cafe was crowded. The synthesizer music pulsed heavily under the noise of the people. Dave strolled through the crowd towards a small table in the corner, and the Princess followed slowly behind him.

A waitress moved through the pools of light and arrived at their table. "What can I get you?"

"I'll have the roast beef platter," said Dave.

"OK," said the waitress. She noted his order and then looked expectantly at the Princess.

"Saturn salad," murmured the Princess.

The waitress floated away. Dave looked at the Princess, but she looked away, watching the crowd. She seemed sullen.

"Are you feeling OK?" asked Dave.

The Princess shrugged and nodded. "Yes, I feel OK," she said.

Dave drummed his fingers on the table. He could tell that something was bothering his girlfriend, but he didn't know what it was or what to do about it. He looked across the table at her. She was sitting very still, looking beyond Dave at some of the people at other tables.

After a long time, the waitress brought them their food. Dave was hungry and dug into his sandwich, but the Princess just picked at her salad.

"You're not eating," said Dave.

"I'm not very hungry," said the Princess.

Dave was becoming convinced that something was wrong. "What's wrong?" he asked.

The Princess nearly tore his head off. "Nothing!" she hissed at him, with fire in her eyes. "Why do you keep asking me that? Everything's fine, OK?"

"Geez, OK," said Dave.

He continued to wonder what was bothering the Princess, but he no longer dared to asked her about it.

Chapter 98

She was asleep.

It was just past 7 pm on a warm, pleasant evening in April, and Lori was asleep. Unfortunately, she was ill—a virus of some kind—and the pills the doctor had given her made her sleepy. The bottle said "Do not drive or operate heavy machinery while using this medication." Actually, the cure seemed worse than the illness; it had wiped her out for the day, and it looked like she would sleep all night as well.

Having just begun dating, Jim savored his first opportunity to serve as a supportive boyfriend. He sat on the edge of the bed, in Lori's room at her apartment, just watching her sleep.

She looked so peaceful, her chest rising and falling with each slow breath. He wanted to touch her, just to let her know he was there, but he was afraid of disturbing her. At last he reached out and gently stroked her hair. She didn't seem to notice.

Outside, children played in the street. About ten of them were out there, running around, laughing and screaming and shouting. The sounds drifted in through the open window on the shoulders of a warm, gentle breeze.

The phone rang, and Jim scrambled to answer it before the noise woke Lori. He picked it up during the second ring and whispered "Hello?"

It was Peter. He said they needed a fourth for Icehouse, and were hoping that Jim might meet them at the Saturn Cafe that evening. Jim gave his regrets, saying that he wanted to spend the evening with his new girlfriend, even though she was sick.

As they talked, Jim was dismayed to see that the sound had woken Lori. She rolled over onto her stomach, and when Jim hung up the phone, he also unplugged it.

He stood by the window, listening to the outdoor sounds and Lori's deep breathing, smelling the wonderful warm spring air, watching as the twilight faded into the blackness of night.

He read the City Paper, and did a sketch of Lori's sleeping shape.

Then Jim felt hungry. He was afraid that cooking would be too noisy, so instead he put on his sandals and went out. He walked up the street to a nearby doughnut shop and got a dozen.

When he got back, Lori was awake. She had crawled out into the living room and was sprawled on the couch, watching television.

"Feeling better?" he asked.

"Yes," she said, as she flashed him one of her trademarked smiles. "What did you bring me?"

"Doughnuts," replied Jim.

Chapter 99

"So," said Dave, "What do you feel like doing tonight?"

They were sitting at the dining room table in the Princess's apartment. She took a sip of her tea and said, "I was thinking about staying home and making a loaf of bread."

This idea didn't exactly thrill Dave. He made a sort of groaning noise. "Well, I suppose we could do that."

The Princess gazed into her teacup. She started to say something, but then stopped. "Umm, I..."

Dave waited for her to say something, but she didn't. "What?" he asked. "What were you going to say?"

"Hmm. What I meant was, I was thinking of staying home and making bread. Alone."

Dave raised his eyebrows. "Oh?"

Suddenly the Princess put her teacup down and stood up. She attempted to say several things at once, but it came out a garbled mess. Then she took a deep breath and sat down again.

"I think we should stop seeing each other," she said.

Dave was too stunned to respond.

After a pause, she said, "I don't think this is really working, at least not for me, and I think it's time we brought it to a close."

Dave took a sudden deep breath. He shook his head slowly from side to side. "I don't-" He paused. "I mean, I'm-" He didn't know what to say, and had basically lost the power of speech.

The Princess pulled her chair up close to him, and put her hand out, touching his. "Listen, now. I do like you. I always have. And it has been fun. But, I just don't think we're quite right for each other."

"What do you mean we're not right for each other? We get along great!"

She shook her head. "No, we don't. We think very differently." She sighed. "Remember the movie, 'Neon Highways'? Remember how we argued about that? And that's just one little example. We fight like that all the time. We can't even eat the same meal! I'm a vegetarian and you don't like vegetables! How are we supposed to get along if we don't even eat the same foods?"

Dave felt his head spinning, he felt dizzy. He thought he was about to fall over.

"And I'll tell you something else," continued the Princess. "Remember a couple of months ago you got a strange black package in the mail? And you got all upset about it and threw it away because you didn't like being told what to do? Remember that?"

Dave nodded slowly.

"I sent you that."

Dave's eyes bulged. "What? Really?"

"Yes! I thought you'd find it funny! But instead you got all mad, because you thought somebody was trying to push you around. So I never felt like telling you it was me."

Dave looked away. He could think of nothing to say.

The Princess sighed heavily, and disappeared into her bedroom. After a moment, she emerged with a small cardboard box. It contained Dave's toothbrush, a couple of books of his which she'd borrowed, a comb, one of his shirts, and an old pair of his socks. She set the box down on the floor near Dave but didn't say anything about it.

She sat down across from him, and they looked at each other.

Dave couldn't believe this was happening. For a long time, they sat silently looking at each other. Dave spent this time thinking, trying to figure out if there were some way he could salvage the relationship. He thought about bringing her flowers, then mentally hit himself for being so shallow. He considered learning to become a vegetarian, but figured she wouldn't believe it anymore than he could deal with it. He wondered if she'd been after a deeper commitment, and considered asking her to marry him; but he decided this was incorrect, and that he'd just humiliate himself if he suggested it.

"What are you thinking?" asked the Princess.

Dave tried to speak, but couldn't. Suddenly the reality of the situation hit him, and he realized it was over. He could do nothing to stop it, and all at once he felt very sad and very alone. He looked into her eyes, and saw that her love for him had died.

He realized that anything he said or did now would be stupid and embarrassing, and he decided it would be better to leave quietly than to humiliate himself by making a scene. So, he resolved to be cool. He shoved his emotions down inside him, down into his stomach. He took a deep breath, and held it, gritting his teeth to hold back his tears. Then he stood up. "I guess this is it then," he said. He picked up the box and walked to the door.

The Princess followed him. He opened the door, and then, standing in the doorway, he turned toward the Princess. "Goodbye," he said, "I'll see you around sometime."

The Princess put her arms around Dave, and they hugged. "Goodbye," she said, "Take care of yourself." Then Dave walked off down the hall, and the Princess shut the door behind him.

When Dave got outside, he leaned against a wall and cried.

After a few minutes, he regained his composure, and examined the contents of the box. He put one of the books into his back pocket, and tossed everything else into a nearby dumpster.

Chapter 100

Dave wandered aimlessly around the streets for about an hour, thinking. Then it began to rain, so he headed for home.

At 9:33 he opened the door to the apartment. Bert was lying on the couch watching television and eating popcorn. Peter and Paul sat at the kitchen table playing Gin Rummy.

"Hey," said Peter, "What happened to you? Figured you'd be with the 'Princess' all night." His tone was mocking. Paul didn't look up from the cards on the table, and Bert mumbled to himself as he changed the channel with the remote control.

"So did I," said Dave, as if in a trance. "But I guess..."

His voice trailed off into silence.

"Hey are you OK?" asked Peter.

"Uh, yeah, I'm fine," said Dave.

"You don't look fine," said Peter. "What happened?"

Dave stared blankly at Peter for a minute, then said "I... I just moved into the Empty City."

Paul looked up at him for the first time with a confused expression on his face. "What?"

"Never mind," said Dave. "You guys want to play a game of Icehouse?"

Nanofiction
55 word short stories

Into the Unknown

When Scorpio-5 landed at Cydonia, few believed they'd find alien artifacts. But they did. The ancient pyramid contained the still-operational inter-dimensional doorway through which the original population had apparently abandoned Mars. But where'd it lead now? Earth? The future? "Empty space" wasn't the answer Commander Thompson expected as he leapt through the portal...

www.wunderland.com/Andy/

Epilogue: The Martian Archeological Society

As Claude stepped out of the men's room and started walking back down the hall to the restaurant where he and some friends were enjoying a few cocktails, he noticed that a certain door was ajar. This door sported a gold plaque with the words "Members Only."

Claude had noticed the door on previous visits to this hotel and had always wondered what went on behind it. Every time before this, of course, the door was sealed up tight, so Claude could only wonder what these mysterious members did. But today, the door was open.

Claude glanced up and down the hallway. No one was in sight. He decided to make the most of this opportunity. He stepped quickly across the hallway and slipped inside the door.

No sooner had he done so that he felt a firm hand upon his chest, guiding him back through the door and out into the hall.

"Sorry," said a voice attached to the hand, "Members Only."

"Members of what?" asked Claude.

The man who owned the voice and the hand stepped out into the hall with Claude and closed the door behind him. "Members of the Martian Archeological Society," he answered tersely. He was a tall man with a thick, bushy, black beard and small oval glasses, dressed in a white suit. He had a little gold pin that looked like a shovel on his lapel.

"Well, how do I join?" persisted Claude.

The man looked sternly at Claude for a moment or two. "I doubt seriously if you'd be admitted," he said at length.

This made Claude angry. "Hey, come on!" he said. "How can you say that when you don't even know me?"

The man shrugged. "Very well, wait one moment while I get you an application." He went back in through the Members Only door and returned a minute later with a little brochure. "Here you are," he said. "This will tell you everything you need to know." He handed it to Claude and went away again, the door closing behind him with a loud click.

Claude looked down at the brochure. "So You Want To Become An Archeologist" it said on the front. He opened it up. Inside he found the following list of membership requirements:

To become a member, you must first pay an application fee of $25.00 (in cash). This fee will not be refunded under any circumstances.

You must then play Martian Chess against 3 members in good standing of the Society. You may play up to 4 games. You must win at least once in order to become a member. This test for membership may not be repeated.

Society members will be available to compete against at 10:00 AM on the first Saturday of every month, in the lobby outside the Member's Lounge.

Members of the organization known as The Children of Mars are not eligible for membership in the Martian Archeological Society.

Below this was a form to be filled out. The rules for Martian Chess appeared on the pages that followed. The brochure contained no more information about the Society itself.

The brochure filled Claude with more questions than it answered, so he knocked on the door of the Member's Lounge. The door stayed closed. He waited a few moments, then gave up.

"Hey, there he is," said Damon as Claude returned to his table. "We were starting to get worried about you."

"Say, guys," said Claude, "what do you know about the Martian Archeological Society?"

Claude's merry band of co-workers collectively had no clue. They shrugged and shook their heads and said "never heard of 'em" sort of things.

"OK, then what about Martian Chess?"

This provoked a similar lack of information, followed by a flurry of counter-questions about why Claude was asking about these things. So he explained about the Members Only door and showed them the brochure. "Anyway," he concluded, "does anyone have an Icehouse set?"

"Yeah, I do," said Larry. "I got it for Christmas last year, but I've never been any good at that game. Why?"

"Can I borrow it? It says here that you need an Icehouse set and a chess board to play Martian Chess."

A couple of people in the group started laughing. One of them said, "What, are you going to try to join their dumb club?"

Claude nodded. "Sure, why not? I've got a couple of weeks to learn the game. How hard can it be?"

Although most of the group seemed to think Claude would be wasting his time, Larry was intrigued. "I'll bring in myset and we can try playing over lunch," he said quietly to Claude. Claude nodded, and then changed the subject to office gossip.

The next day at lunch, Claude and Larry took over an empty conference room and taught themselves to play Martian Chess. The game involved using nine Icehouse pyramids for each player, of an assortment of different colors, in the corners of a chessboard.

The large size pyramids were called Queens and worked like Queens; the middle size pyramids were called Drones and moved like Rooks, except only up to two spaces at a time; and the small pyramids were called Pawns and moved like Bishops except only one space at a time.

The object was simply to capture as many enemy pieces as possible, as they were worth points at the end of the game, with the larger pieces being more valuable.

The trick was that instead of knowing which pieces were yours by their color, you instead controlled all of the pieces in your section of the board. When you moved a piece out of your part of the board, you lost control of it, and when someone else moved a piece into your space, it became your piece. It was a very unpredictable game.

Claude and Larry quickly realized that the game would be much more complex with four players, and since the membership test required that they win four player games, they needed others to play with. It was obvious that no one else in the Happy Hour crowd would be interested, so they asked around among others in the office to find out who else liked games. They pretty quickly found three or four others, and soon they'd gotten quite a regular lunch time gaming session going. And the more they played, the better they got at the game.

The first Saturday of the month was soon upon them, but Larry and Claude felt confident that they'd be good enough to get in.

The lobby was relatively crowded, but not packed. Overall, there seemed to be about fifteen people applying for membership and only around a dozen society members, so it took a little while for Larry and Claude's turns to come up. As they waited, they watched some of the earlier arrivals play their games.

One thing they noticed right away was that the game sets being used here had pyramids that were all of a single color, unlike the random mix of colors the rules had told them to use.

"Well," said Larry, after thinking about it for a moment, "color is meaningless in Martian Chess. If you've only got one Icehouse set, then the best way to de-emphasize color is for everyone to start with an assortment of the colors in the set. I suppose it's even better to use pieces that are all the same color, but you'd need three identical Icehouse stashes in order to do that."

At last, Claude was called, and he sat down in front of his opponents. Two were women, one in her late twenties and one who appeared to be at least sixty. The third was a kid, a boy of no more than twelve years of age. All three wore gold shovel pins. They smiled at Claude and greeted him warmly, but Claude had a sinking feeling as he sat down at the table. Claude felt there were sharp teeth behind those pleasant smiles.

He was right. They tore him apart. The first three games were over quickly, and Claude was the big loser in all three.

The older lady said gently, "If you'd like, we can stop here. You can save your last game and try again some other day, after you improve."

Claude's high spirits had already been too badly crushed. He decided to go ahead and get his last game over with, rather than to try again and waste some other Saturday morning. He lost that game as well.

Claude waited around for Larry to finish up his games, and was surprised when he came bouncing excitedly over to him. "Well, I'm in!" he said, beaming. "The first two games were brutal, but I learned a lot from them and I won my third game. How you'd do?"

"I got crushed," said Claude, dejected.

"Oh, bummer man! Well, I've gotta go to some sort of new member briefing now. I'll see you on Monday!"

Claude went home depressed. But after a while, he cheered up a bit. His main goal in trying to join was to find out what goes on in the Member's Lounge. Well, he may not get to see it for himself, but at least now he knew a member he could shake down for the information.

On Monday morning, Claude went almost directly over to Larry's desk. "So, Mr. Archeologist, tell me all about it!"

Larry smiled sheepishly. "I knew you were going to ask me this," he replied, "but I gotta say up front that there are some things I'm supposed to keep secret."

Claude rolled his eyes. "Oh, great! Well, what can you tell me?"

Larry shrugged. "Well, what do you want to know?"

"Well, for starters, what's in the Member's Lounge?"

Larry shook his head. "I can't tell you."

"Oh, great, that's just great," said Claude, very annoyed.

There was an awkward silence. Larry looked at his computer screen. "Listen," he said, "let's go to lunch later and I'll tell you what I can."

"Fine," said Claude. And he wandered off.

Larry and Claude went out for lunch. They didn't say much until they were outside, walking along the street.

"OK," said Larry, "Here's the deal. Have you heard of the Children of Mars?"

Claude scratched his head. "No, except for on that brochure."

"Yeah, I hadn't either. But they told us all about them on Saturday. Basically, the Children of Mars is this club that you can only get into if you have red hair. It was started by the guy who created Icehouse and he's got all these absurd ideas about how redheads are descended from people who came here from Mars centuries ago. It doesn't seem like the club has any real point, though, except to be an exclusive club."

"I don't get it," said Claude. "What do they have to do with the Archeologists?"

"Nothing," said Larry. "That's the whole point. That's why the Martian Archeological Society was created in the first place. See, a bunch of people who didn't have red hair decided that, since they couldn't get into the Children of Mars, they'd start their own club and refuse to let anybody with red hair join it. But since they also wanted it to be an exclusive, 'members only' sort of club, they came up with a different sort of test, namely the chess game, to decide who could join."

Claude was still confused. "If they don't want to have anything to do with the Children of Mars, then why do they call themselves Martian Archeologist and play Martian Chess and stuff like that?"

"Because they consider the Children of Mars the enemy, that's why. That's what the name is all about. One of their big things is that they want the Space Agency to do a manned mission to Mars that can prove, once and for all, that there isn't and never has been any life on Mars. The only way to destroy the Children of Mars as a group is to prove that their whole premise is false, and the only way to do that is to send archeologists to Mars to look for signs of the supposed long-dead civilization. So the name of the organization is kind of wrong... it really should be the Society of Aspiring Martian Archeologists, or something like that. "

"OK, fine. But what about the game?"

"One of the founders created it. He decided he didn't want to play Icehouse anymore since he was being discriminated against by the Children of Mars, so he came up with a new game that he could play with his Icehouse set. He called it Martian Chess because he wanted to make fun of the Children of Mars."

"How's that?"

"Well, they have this race-memory theory, which says that Icehouse is actually an ancient Martian game, which was 'rediscovered' by tapping into these old race-memories that people with red hair have. So, I guess the guy who created Martian Chess was hoping to get the Children of Mars pissed off, by claiming to have 'rediscovered' an old Martian thing even though he's not a redhead."

"Did it work?"

Larry shrugged. "I dunno."

They walked along in silence for a few minutes.

"OK, fine,." said Claude. "So what happens in the Lounge?"

"It's just a private lounge," said Larry. "It's not all that interesting, really."

"Then tell me about it!" pleaded Claude.

Larry shook his head. "Sorry, I can't. It's a secret."

Claude sighed. He could tell that Larry wouldn't tell him no matter how much he nagged, so he gave up. He fantasized for awhile about trying to break into the lounge, and then about dying his hair and trying to join the Children of Mars. After this, he started fantasizing about one of his co-workers, and tried to put both of these so-called Martian organizations out of his mind.

Then one day, a few weeks later, Claude heard about a coffeeshop over on Iceland street, right across from the Saturn Cafe, where they played yet another game with Icehouse pieces. The place was called Planet X-33, the game they played there was called Zarcana...

Nanofiction
55 word short stories

It Happened When He Played the Tower

Planet X-33 kept an assortment of tarot decks on hand for use by customers. To avoid karmic contamination, some were stored with the Icehouse sets, others with the Ouija boards. But one evening, a deck from the Ouija Lounge wound up at a Zarcana table. The game ended prematurely, due to a mysterious power outage.

www.wunderland.com/Andy/

Author's Notes

I wrote the short story "The Empty City" (which is credited to Jim in chapter 43) back in 1985, for a creative writing class in college. Although I was studying to be a computer scientist, my dream was to become a writer someday. After college, I got a job programming computers for NASA, but in my spare time, I wrote stories.

About two years later, while myself living in the Empty City, I wrote a really long short story, entitled "Icehouse" (which later become Chapters 2-33 of the book you now hold in your hands). Although my friends very much enjoyed the story, what they really wanted was that game with little pyramids. Unfortunately, neither the game nor the pyramids you needed to play it with were real.

But my friends weren't going to let that stop them. Little pyramids can be made by hand in various ways, and soon we were learning the arcane art of Game Design by trial and error. It was John Cooper who first figured out a real game based on my concepts, and that first game proved so compelling we didn't invent any others for over seven years. Indeed, I have seen real people play the real game of Icehouse with every bit as much intensity and seriousness as the characters in this book. (There's no better example of this than the Icehouse tournament at our annual "Big Experiment" at Origins each summer.)

But it all might have stopped there if it weren't for another friend of mine, a co-worker at NASA named Kristin. Not only did Kristin become my ticket out of the Empty City, but also my partner in what would become a career I had never even imagined for myself. Instead of being a writer, I became a professional game designer. With Kristin's entrepreneurial drive, we started a company and eventually quit our high-tech jobs to become full-time game-makers.

In the fall of 1999, after gaining success with easier-to-produce games like Fluxx and Aquarius, we finally began production on the beautiful, crystalline Icehouse pyramids we had dreamed of making for so very long. Never could I have imagined, when I wrote that first story about a game with little pyramids, that I would someday see beautiful pyramids in real-life, just like the ones I'd described, being mass produced in a factory. Nor could I have foreseen that my imaginary game would become not just an actual game, but a whole series of different games as varied and exciting as those you can play with a standard deck of cards.

With so many different games available now for the pyramids, everyone has their own list of favorites. Here are my current top five:

- **Volcano:** It's my all-time favorite game to play at a restaurant.
- **IceTowers:** If you use giant cardboard pyramids, it becomes a sport!
- **Icehouse:** Yes, even after all these years, I still love the original game.
- **Zarcana:** I prefer it over the similar-but-more-aggressive Gnostica.
- **RAMbots:** I won the tournament at the Big Experiment in 2002!

It's so hard choosing just five, though... I'm also a big fan of Homeworlds, and many Icehouse fans would choose Zendo as their all-time favorite. But this is why we've included a full dozen of the best Icehouse games in our book, *Playing with Pyramids*. Look for it wherever Icehouse Pieces are sold.

If you'd like to read more of my writings, please visit our weekly webzine, which we updated each Thursday at Wunderland.com. Among the many things you'll find there is an essay entitled "Playing Hearts with Pyramids," in which I discuss my preferred rules for Hearts, my favorite classic card game. It was the experience long ago of playing endless games of Hearts with the same group of guys that first inspired these stories about an imaginary game, and in a wonderful example of things coming full circle, I now use Icehouse pyramids to keep score when I play the game that inspired Icehouse. (The system we use is described on the next page.)

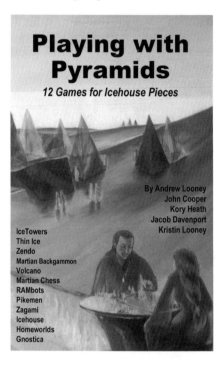

Playing with Pyramids

12 Games for Icehouse Pieces

By Andrew Looney
John Cooper
Kory Heath
Jacob Davenport
Kristin Looney

IceTowers
Thin Ice
Zendo
Martian Backgammon
Volcano
Martian Chess
RAMbots
Pikemen
Zagami
Icehouse
Homeworlds
Gnostica

Anyway, I hope you enjoyed this book. For those of you with someone to love, I hope these stories have reminded you of how wonderful it is not to be alone. And for those of you living now in Empty Cities of your own, here's hoping that soon you'll find someone special who can stamp your exit visa...

ANDY

Scoring with Pyramids

Icehouse pieces are so wonderfully versatile that you can even use them to solve an age-old problem faced by game-players of every stripe: keeping score. Instead of fussing about with paper and pencil, why not keep score using a bowlful of beautiful pyramids?

Here's how it works: Contrary to their typical values, large Icehouse pieces are worth 10 points, the mediums are worth 5, and the smalls are worth 1. With 15 pieces in a standard stash, that gives you 80 points to work with for each player. (If the game has an end condition that depends on someone reaching, say, 100 points, just change that number to 80. It will make for a slightly shorter game, but that really shouldn't matter since stopping at 100 points is just as arbitrary.)

If the goal of the game is to gain points, the pyramids will start in the bowl and be paid out to players as needed. On the other hand, if the goal is to avoid points (as in Hearts), then each player will start with an allotment of points (i.e. one standard stash) and will lose pyramids (paying them into the bowl) in accordance with points taken. When someone runs out of pyramids, the game ends (just as when someone's score reaches the game-ending limit).

In a game like Hearts, where a fixed total number of points are collected after each round, the sacrificed pyramids can be piled in the center and counted before going into the bowl. This allows for a check that all points have been accounted for, and also facilitates making change.

Sometimes you just won't have the right combination of pyramids in front of you, and you'll need to receive change. Because of this, all pieces being paid out will be placed *upright* in the center of the table, with returning change being placed *lying down*. As long as all players follow this format, the score totals for each round can easily be verified before the pyramids move on to their final destinations.

So, if you'd like to spend more time playing the game and less time keeping score (or if you can't write down the scores because you're an orthodox Jew and it's the Sabbath), then trying keeping score using Icehouse pieces. It's fast, it's easy, and it doesn't waste paper!

Nanofiction
55 word short stories

The Agony of Defeat

A crowd formed around the Zarcana table as word of the high stakes game spread throughout the coffeehouse. Gambling wasn't really permitted at Planet X-33, but this was different: with news of their father's ailing health on their minds, four siblings were settling a question of great importance to them all. Tonight's stakes: one kidney.

www.wunderland.com/Andy/

Credits

Andrew Looney wrote most of the stories in this book between 1985 and 1991, and his personality (at that point in his life) is reflected in the book's characters, many of whom are based on Andy and on other real people he knew at the time. Like Jim, Andy was once an aspiring writer looking for romance, who dabbled in photography, mailed random objects to random people, and vastly preferred long-haired women who don't wear makeup to those who follow the whims of the fashion industry. The Four are based on a real gaming group Andy once played Hearts with incessantly (also occasionally engaging in bizarre late-night shenanigans), and reflects Andy's belief that game-playing should be a constant part of life. As the real-life inventor of Icehouse (first imagined in Chapter 2 of this book), Andy based the character of the Emperor of Mars on his notions of who he might be in the future: an eccentric hermit whose fridge is stocked with nothing but soda, TV dinners, and frozen desserts. (The character of Doctor Cool is likewise based on John Cooper, who refined the rules to the original game – and who at that time favored motorcycles and black leather.) Like Torrence, Andy is a cartoonist who has always been fascinated with underground secret hideouts and bomb shelters. Andy's dream of traveling through time is fulfilled by Bill, his fascination with all things Martian is reflected in the strange subculture of the Children of Mars, and his favorite food (chocolate angel-food cake) is served at Dollars to Donuts. Andy's design aesthetics are seen in his descriptions of their fully encloseable booths, not to mention the retro-modern-interplanetary decor of the Saturn Cafe, lit with pools of light and permeated by the sounds of ambient synthesized music. And like the Martian Princess, Andy habitually carries a Stardust in his pocket.

Alison Frane never would have imagined, back when she first read this book, that she'd someday be living with the author and illustrating a new edition. At the time (1999), *The Empty City* was being republished on the internet, one chapter per week, and Alison was glued to her computer each week when the next chapter appeared online. After realizing it would take almost a year before getting to the end, she decided she couldn't wait and bought a copy of the cheap first edition which was available at the time. Besides artwork, Alison loves plants, words, esoteric knowledge, and helping stuffed animals talk.

Dawn Robyn Petrlik painted the cover for this book so long ago, it was before Andy and Kristin got married. Now she lives in Brooklyn, NY with a pit bull named Mona, and gets paid to paint and draw.